PRAISE FOR

The Canyon's Edge

A Chicago Public Library Best of the Best Book

A *Kirkus Reviews* Best Children's Book

An NCTE Notable Verse Novel

"**A powerful, heart-thumping story**
about survival and the inner strength it takes to
reclaim life after trauma. Nora shows us that it's
possible to emerge stronger than we've ever
been before." —Ann Braden, award-winning author
of *The Benefits of Being an Octopus*

"You won't be able to stop turning pages of this
gripping, unforgettable novel with
emotional depth and resonance as you cheer for
Nora to conquer her inner and outer beasts."
—Donna Gephart, award-winning author of *Lily and
Dunkin*, *The Paris Project*, and *Abby, Tried and True*

"A **haunting, heart-pounding** story of
survival, brilliantly told in verse. *The Canyon's Edge*
will inspire, uplift and resonate. I loved it!"
—Barbara Dee, author of *Maybe He Just Likes You*
and *My Life in the Fish Tank*

THE
CANYON'S
EDGE

THE CANYON'S EDGE

DUSTI BOWLING

LITTLE, BROWN AND COMPANY
New York Boston

Copyright © 2020 by Dusti Bowling
Excerpt from *Across the Desert* copyright © 2021 by Dusti Bowling

Cover art copyright © 2020 by Pascal Campion
Cover design by Karina Granda
Interior design by Carla Weise
Cover copyright © 2020 by Hachette Book Group, Inc.

Art on pages iii, vii, 165, 303: © Nikiparonak/Shutterstock.com;
v: © aksol/Shutterstock.com; 78: © Digital Bazaar/Shutterstock.com;
90: © Olga Rom/Shutterstock.com; 97: © Sudowoodo/Shutterstock.com;
163: © Naddya/Shutterstock.com; 196: © Sabelskaya/Shutterstock.com;
209, 223: © aksol/Shutterstock.com; 237: © Morphart Creation/Shutterstock.com;
257: © 3dlibrary/Shutterstock.com; 269: © moj0j0/Shutterstock.com

Little, Brown and Company
Hachette Book Group
1290 Avenue of the Americas, New York, NY 10104
Visit us at LBYR.com

Originally published in hardcover and ebook by Little, Brown and Company in September 2020
First Trade Paperback Edition: September 2021

Little, Brown and Company is a division of Hachette Book Group, Inc. The Little, Brown name and logo are trademarks of Hachette Book Group, Inc.

The publisher is not responsible for websites (or their content) that are not owned by the publisher.

The Library of Congress has cataloged the hardcover edition as follows:
Names: Bowling, Dusti, author.
Title: The canyon's edge / Dusti Bowling.
Description: First edition. | New York : Little, Brown and Company, 2020. | Audience: Ages 8–12. |
Summary: A year after the death of her mother in a restaurant shooting, Nora is left struggling to stay alive when a climbing trip with her father goes terribly wrong.
Identifiers: LCCN 2019054068 | ISBN 9780316494694 (hardcover) | ISBN 9780316494687 (ebook) | ISBN 9780316494656 (ebook)
Subjects: CYAC: Novels in verse. | Survival—Fiction. | Post-traumatic stress disorder—Fiction. | Hiking—Fiction. | Canyons—Fiction. | Family life—Fiction.
Classification: LCC PZ7.5.B695 Can 2020 | DDC [Fic]—dc23
LC record available at https://lccn.loc.gov/2019054068

ISBNs: 978-0-316-49467-0 (pbk.),
978-0-316-49468-7 (ebook)

Printed in the United States of America

LSC-H

Printing 4, 2022

FOR MY MOM

PART ONE

ONE

I walk to the Jeep in the middle of a cold, dark desert night. Dad is already stuffing our supplies into the back, the tailpipe blowing steam tinted red by taillights. We need an early start; it's going to take a while to reach the place where no one can find us.

Dad lifts a hand and pats my rumpled hair. "Tired?" he asks.

I nod.

He pushes my backpack toward me. "Why don't you double-check it?" I open my bag as Dad digs through his own and mumbles, "It feels like I'm missing something."

His words hit me right in the chest. We *are* missing something. We'll always be missing something.

Shivering, I zip up my pink hoodie, which I got at Sunset Crater. It says *Get Out There*, but this is the first time we'll be "getting out there" since our family went from three to two.

Pushing those thoughts away, I sort through the supplies Dad put in my pack: water bottles, sunblock, helmet, almonds, protein bars, and my favorite flavor of electrolyte powder, watermelon. He remembers.

I smile up at him, but he's now ripping everything out of his pack. "I know I'm forgetting something," he says, his voice rising. He pulls out rope for rappelling, cams for climbing, carabiners for carrying, gloves for gripping, and harnesses to hold us.

Touching his arm, I say, "I think we have everything," though it feels like a lie. He continues emptying his pack until he pulls out one last item: gun.

I stumble backward, choking on my own breath.

Dad looks back at me and immediately sets it down. He takes me into his arms, much thinner than they used to be. "I'm sorry, Nora," he whispers. "It's just a flare gun."

My heart pounds so hard I'm sure Dad can feel it.

"I doubt we'd ever need to use it," Dad says, patting my back. "Hey, it's gonna be a good day."

I take in a deep breath. "I know."

Dad looks up. "Almost no moon," he says. "Did you hear about those bones they found on the moon?"

My head snaps back. "What?"

He grins. "I guess the cow didn't make it."

I groan. "Oh my gosh, Dad."

He gives my long hair a gentle tug, then stuffs everything back in his pack and slams the hatch shut. He limps around to the driver's side and gets in. He seems more like himself today than in a very long time. It really might be a good day.

TWO

We drive the empty desert highway for a couple of hours until Dad turns onto a rough dirt road that follows the power lines. I slide my hand across the foggy window and peer through the wet streaks. Nothing but desert surrounds us as we drive—no homes, no people, no cars except ours. Nothing but ocotillos, saguaros, mesquites, palo verdes, and wolf spiders with eyes that shine like diamonds in our headlights. Dad points them out to me.

"You see that one?"

I scan the lit area. "Yep."

"There's another one."

"I see it."

Dad thinks wolf spiders are amazing.

"You should have invited Danielle," he says suddenly.

I swallow, thinking about the last time we were all together, when we went camping and fishing at Bartlett Lake. How I had to hook all her worms because Danielle didn't want to touch them. How she'd squealed in excitement at catching the smallest bluegill ever. How Mom had snapped a picture of it. How I threw it back in the water and Danielle had jumped in after it, yelling that she'd wanted to keep it as a pet. How I jumped in after her, and we spent the rest of the day swimming and splashing and scaring away the fish.

"Sorry," Dad says. "I just...miss her. That's all."

I miss her, too, though I can't bring myself to say it out loud.

THREE

It's dawn by the time Dad stops, startling me awake. It was a quick nap, and I try to hold on to the dream, but it's already gone.

If it had been the nightmare, I would still feel it. I wouldn't be able to forget.

Dad turns off the Jeep and the lights blink out. I step into the cold morning and stretch, run my fingers through my long hair, and pull it back in a ponytail. The sun is rising behind the dark line of mountains, their tops jagged like the edge of a serrated knife. I reach back into the car and pull out my notebook and pencil and quickly jot down:

The sapphire sky
breathes in
the desert morning
and breathes out
pink flame to burn up
the wisps of silver clouds.

I stuff the notepad and pencil in my backpack. When Mary, my therapist, found out I liked writing, she told me I should use it as a tool—that I could rewrite my nightmare. But I don't want to do that. Rewriting it means I have to think about it. What I want is to crumple it up and throw it in the garbage, burn it, delete it forever. But Mary wasn't totally wrong. Writing makes me feel closer to Mom, like I can somehow make up for all the things she'll never write with my poems, though I don't think I could ever write as well as she did.

"Maybe you could read me what you're writing later," Dad says.

"Maybe."

"It would be nice to share it with someone, don't you think?"

"I don't know. Maybe it's just for me."

Shrugging, Dad slips his backpack on and buckles

it around his chest and waist. He runs a hand through his graying hair, overgrown and curling over his ears, then locks the Jeep. We set out away from the road, our hiking boots crunching over the hard desert dirt.

I'm still sleepy, and I stumble over a couple of larger rocks.

"Watch your step," Dad says, but he should be paying attention to his own steps—he's stumbling more than I am.

I watch him limp, knowing every step hurts. Every night, he rubs his leg with special lotion. Every month, he visits the doctor. Every day, he swallows pills. Three surgeries and a metal rod. Nice words like *I'm okay* and *I feel fine*, but I know he's still in pain. It will never go away.

A bullet can do that.

A bullet is tiny. It can weigh a fraction of an ounce and be a fraction of an inch long. And yet, something that small can rip flesh and shatter bone and puncture organs and stop hearts. Something that small can tear a hole in your life so large it will never close, so ragged it will never be sewn, so ugly no one will ever look at you the same again, so painful you'll feel it every second for the rest of your life.

Even when that tiny bullet never touched you at all.

FOUR

We stop after a few minutes, and Dad checks his map and com-
pass. I gaze at the mountains to the west now that
the sky has brightened, but the sun hasn't yet reached
them—it's still really dark over there.

"Well," Dad says, and I turn to him. "We go this
way." He folds up the map and points to the east.

It's quiet except for the skittering of small lizards
and the *ah, ah, ah, ah, ah, ah* of a cactus wren—the
sound like an engine that won't turn over. Surrounded
by nothing but the cold waking desert, I feel the rising
sun heat my face. I'm both cool and warm, worried
yet hopeful, loving and hating, at peace and at war.

We hike to the top of a small hill, and I get my first glimpse of the canyon.

Mom, Dad, and I once watched a documentary about a man who walked over a canyon on a tightrope. Despite knowing he wouldn't fall, I was as tense as the rope he walked on. This last year has felt that way—like I'm walking a tightrope. Or maybe like I *am* the tightrope. I told Mary this. She responded: "Eleanor"—she calls me Eleanor, even though everyone else calls me Nora—"you're not the tightrope. You're the canyon. And your healing is like the water carving you. It takes time. It's a never-ending process. But as you heal and grow, something beautiful and layered and solid and lasting is formed."

I think Mary might be a poet, too.

FIVE

Dad and I finally reach the edge of the isolated, unnamed canyon he found for us. It's narrow, widening and tapering, twisting and turning as far as I can see. Looking down into it is like getting a peek at an unknown world. I can only see the bottom in snippets, some of it hidden by the curving walls or outcroppings, some of it so dark that anything could be waiting in the shadows. The walls I do see are layered and look as though they've been burned in places. That's the desert's varnish. On the other side, maybe only fifteen feet across, a kangaroo rat scampers to the edge, seems to be inspecting the canyon, too.

"Cool!" I say. "It's a slot canyon."

The only other slot canyon I'd been to was Antelope Canyon, and that one had been packed with tourists. I'd wanted to take my time exploring every hidden crack and corner, every layer cut and carved by wind and water, but our guide had rushed us through.

"Yep," Dad says, clearly impressed with himself. "Hard to find, too. Took lots of expert research." He leans over and looks down into the crevice, whistling. "Isn't she a beauty?"

"It's actually pretty small." I grin. "Honestly, it's not all that impressive."

Dad presses a hand to his chest as if I've hurt him to his core. Then he picks up a rock and tosses it over the canyon. It bounces on the other side in a puff of dust and sends the kangaroo rat scurrying under a nearby brittlebush. "You know, Nora, I think you could jump it."

I laugh. "Yeah, right."

"So it's not *that* small, then?"

I shake my head. "It's medium at best."

Snickering, Dad unbuckles his backpack and tosses it on the ground. He pulls out our rope and harnesses while I secure my helmet. Dad finds a good-sized boulder at the edge and sets an anchor in it, then two backup cams in case the anchor fails. He raises a finger and says matter-of-factly, "Redundancy is essential."

Raising a finger, I finish, "Especially when risking your life." We smile at each other, and I don't think we've felt this normal in a year—one year exactly today.

Dad threads the rope and ties stopper knots. We trade our hiking boots for rock shoes and step into our harnesses. I tighten mine around my waist, but Dad still double-checks it.

Dad backs away from me. He stands at an angle on the edge of the canyon, his rope going taut, and a moment of hesitation, of fear, crosses his face. This is the first time since Before. Since his shot leg. Since it's only the two of us instead of the three of us. Then the moment of fear passes. His face lightens. "To infinity and beyond!" he cries, lowering down.

I stand at the edge, watching him. It's obvious how hard it is for him to rappel down by himself. With no one holding the rope at the bottom to help him, he has to control his own descent, slowly threading the rope through the descender, his face twisting in pain and determination—no, it's defiance. No one's a better climber than my dad, and I know that when he makes it to the bottom, he'll feel even more normal again. I want him to be normal again. I want him to be like he used to be.

Slipping gloves over my shaking hands, my stomach clenches. Forty feet. It may not seem like a lot, but it's enough to kill us, especially out here where no one can find us. But Dad doesn't see it that way. In Dad's mind, the only danger in the world is people. This canyon is safety.

Dad wasn't always like this. It started as only one person and one place he feared. But it spread until it became all people and all places. One minute we were tossing boxes of macaroni and cheese into a grocery cart. The next minute we were hiding in the cereal aisle behind a tower of Frosted Flakes on sale, our cart abandoned, Dad shaking, his arms gripped so tightly around me I could barely breathe. After that, Dad kept seeing more and more suspicious people. Kept looking for exits, paths of escape, routes to freedom.

Now our quiet house, this empty desert, the many barriers we've built between us and others—it's all Frosted Flakes on sale.

Dad glances up at me and forces a smile through his sweat and strain. I smile back, trying to assure him with my expression that I'm not worried, that he's doing just fine.

Mary says Dad and I have built walls around ourselves. She says our walls are made of all the unhealthy things—guilt and shame and fear and anger. She says we haven't fully processed or accepted what happened.

But how could anyone accept such a thing? Why shouldn't we build walls to protect ourselves? Mary says the walls are weak, leaky, full of holes that constantly drip and seep pain.

I think maybe we just need to build stronger walls.

SIX

Dad waves from the bottom, and I pull the rope up. Threading the end through my belay loop, I tie my figure-eight knot. Then I thread the rope through again, following the same path, duplicating the pattern, my hands relaxing, my stomach unclenching a little bit. At home I keep a length of rope next to my bed. Sometimes I sit and tie the figure eight for hours.

I grip the rope in my gloved hands, sweat dripping down my back. My hoodie is already too warm. My breath hitches as I step backward off the edge.

"On rappel!" I shout, pushing my legs against the stone, beginning my descent, using my guide hand to feed the rope through the rappel device. The harness straps dig into my lower back and bare legs, and I wish I'd worn long pants instead of jean shorts.

Dad is my belayer, holding the rope at the bottom. He helps keep me steady as I walk backward down the wall, my feet pressed against the rock, the rest of my body leaning into a seated position. One step at a time. Down the wall. My body senses the danger in what I'm doing, and I freeze.

Fear fills me, churns my insides, overwhelms me, makes my mind want to escape to somewhere else, into my poetry. I don't look down. Instead, I focus on the wall in front of me:

> *Layers, layers, and layers.*
> *Smooth pale seams*
> *upon rough spatters of rainbow red*
> *upon pitted and pockmarked pink*
> *upon veins of gray.*
> *Layers, layers, and layers.*

Mary's words break through: *Identify what you fear, Eleanor.*

"Dying," I whisper.

Are you likely to die in this situation?

"No."

Don't leave until you're calm. Facing fear is a skill that must be learned.

I breathe in deep and steady, trying to slow my pounding heart, willing my frozen limbs to move.

"Everything okay up there?" Dad calls, sounding winded from his descent.

Taking another deep breath, I shout, "I'm coming down."

He won't, can't, climb up to help me right now. And I don't expect him to. In the Before, I once froze against another wall. In the Before, Dad climbed up to meet me. In the Before, Dad put his forehead to mine and told me *It's okay. I'm here. Whatever's coming, we'll face it together.*

In the After, Dad doesn't have the strength. In the After, I face this by myself.

SEVEN

Dad pats my helmet and removes it. "I was worried about you for a second. Everything all right?"

I gaze around at the tall, layered walls in every shade of red imaginable and breathe in the cool canyon air. "Yeah." I remove my helmet and clip it to my backpack. "Everything's good."

We change back into our hiking boots. Leaving the bright red rappelling rope in place so we can climb up later, we set off to discover whatever secret things might be hidden down here in the canyon.

I stretch my arms out wide and gently run my fingertips along the canyon walls while I walk. Small embedded pebbles tickle my fingertips and gently chip at my bitten nails. "Hey, Dad." I stop and press my palms against the cool, rough surface. He turns around. "Look, I'm as wide as a canyon."

"As wide as a *small* canyon."

"Well, I didn't say I was as wide as the *Grand* Canyon."

Every passing minute brings more light into this narrow crack in the desert. Rock surrounds us and colors transform, light pink blending into deeper maroon like someone swirled cream into the stone but not very well. Sunlight gradually creeps down one wall of the canyon, the rock shining so brightly above us, it seems the canyon is making the light instead of reflecting it.

"Do you think anything lives down here?" I ask.

Dad points at a small, shallow cave, at the white stains running down the rock. "Bats. Probably smaller animals, lizards, snakes for sure."

"What about bigger animals? Like a mountain lion?"

"I suppose a mountain lion could climb down here."

"Have you ever seen a mountain lion?"

"Yes, but only from a safe distance."

"Is there anything you've never seen in the desert you think would be cool to see?" Mom and Dad spent so much time out here together, it's hard for me to believe there's anything he hasn't seen.

"Oh, sure. Lots of animals." Dad stops and thinks a moment. "Never seen a ringtail. Never seen a fox. That would be pretty neat."

Making our way through the canyon, I gaze up at the pale green jojoba and brittlebush lining the edge and spot a barrel cactus growing out of the wall, where no plant should be able to live. Nothing could ever hurt us down here. Down here we are safe. Alone.

But I'm not sure all this safety is worth all this aloneness.

Dad picks up a rock. "It's shaped like a heart," he says and places it in my hand. "A heart for you, my dear." I roll my eyes at him, and he laughs.

When he turns away, I pocket the heart-shaped stone, the only gift Dad has given me today for my birthday. And this canyon is the only place he can take me because Dad no longer feels any place is safe if people are there— not stores, concerts, festivals, schools, and especially not restaurants. That's why he found us this canyon—because nothing can hurt us when no one is nearby.

We didn't die with Mom one year ago at Café Ardiente, but we've been slowly dying ever since. Alone.

I pat the heart-shaped stone in my pocket and
watch my father's beaming face as he points out a small
gopher snake hiding under a ledge. When he continues walking, I realize he's *humming*. I stop and listen,
finally making out what it is: "Across the Universe."

Maybe today we begin to come back to life.

EIGHT

We stop after several hours of hiking and exploring. I remove my backpack and stretch my arms above me, take out my hair tie, and run my hands over my scalp, sore from my tight ponytail. I toss my hair tie in my pack.

Dad's already munching on some beef jerky, so I grab a protein bar and make my way to an outcropping along one canyon wall where the rock juts out like a small stage a few feet high and wide. I pull myself up and sit cross-legged, eating my bar, running a finger along a deep crack in the stone surface. When I'm done, I take off my hoodie and bunch it up under my head. I lie back on the flat stone surface, just large enough to hold me with my knees bent, and gaze at the slim river of blue sky above. It must be around midday because the desert is quiet and sunlight shines down pretty far into the canyon. Lifting a hand, my fingers nearly touch the beam of light, sparkling with dust, but it's just out of reach.

Pushing off the outcropping and walking over to my backpack, I remove my notebook and sit down next to Dad. He peers over my shoulder, and I pull my notebook up to my chest so he can't spy on what I'm writing. He smiles. "Are you ever going to let me read what you write?"

Hugging my notebook, I tell him, "Maybe."

Dad stares down at me. "Maybe?"

"What if it's not good?"

Dad puts his arm around me. "If it came from your heart, then it can't be anything but good."

"You have to say that. You're my dad," I say, my voice hoarse.

"I mean it. Plus, I have some great lines for you to write."

Raising an eyebrow, I look up at him. "What?"

"What's brown and sticky?"

I squint at him. "What?"

He picks up a small twig from the canyon floor and places it on my knee. "A stick."

Scrunching up my nose and covering my smile with one hand, I brush the twig off my leg.

"Seriously, though," he says, "I used to like writing haikus."

"I like haikus."

Dad scratches his stubbly chin. "If I tell you one, you have to tell me one."

"Okay."

Dad taps a finger to one pale cheek, already turning pink from the morning sun. A mischievous grin builds on his face, and I know whatever's coming is not going to be a serious haiku. "This canyon is small," he says. "But it's way way way bigger," he counts on his fingers as he talks, "than shrimpy Nora."

I roll my eyes. "Seriously, Dad?"

"What?"

"How can you expect me to share my writing when you make a joke out of it?"

"I'm sorry." His grin fades. "I'd still like to hear one if you're willing to share it."

I don't have to make one up on the spot; I have several written in my notebook. The truth is I love writing haikus. They feel orderly…patterned. I often use them to remember the things Mary tells me. Flipping through my notebook, I find one. My choice is not random. My choice is entirely deliberate.

"Hypervigilance," I say. "Dad won't let me go to school." I slowly look up at him. "He's protecting me."

Dad gazes down at me, eyebrows drawn together, questioning, though he doesn't speak. I know he was expecting me to make up something on the spot, and now he's waiting for an explanation.

"I want to go back to school," I say so softly it's nearly a whisper.

Dad's arm falls from my shoulders. He gets up, walks to a canyon wall, facing away from me. He presses one hand to the stone, leans forward, head down, his shaggy hair falling in his face. He breathes in and out as if it's a tremendous effort, then slowly begins to shake his head. He turns to me, not even a trace of smile left. "No."

NINE

My heart pounds and rage swells. That's how my emotions work since Mom died. I go from fine to anxious to depressed to angry to numb in split-second bursts. I grit my teeth. "Can't we even talk about it?"

"No."

"Why?"

"You know why. You read the news, even though I tell you not to."

"So is this how it's going to be? Just me and you, hiding forever?"

"We're not hiding."

"Then what would you call it?" I snap.

"Staying safe."

"Staying safe *alone*."

"We're not alone," Dad pleads. "We have each other."

"I need more than just you." Dad looks hurt at my words, but he must, he *must*, understand that I can love him and still need more than him in my life. "I want to have friends again."

"I told you you should have invited Danielle," he says, voice rising, accusing.

"Danielle doesn't want to be my friend anymore!" I cry. "I have to go where I can make new friends. Where people won't just see the shooting when they look at me. I want to do more with my life than hide. I want things to go back to normal."

"Normal, Nora?" He stares at the ground, his shoulders slumping. Then he lifts his eyes to mine. "How could things ever go back to normal?"

"Maybe if you let me go to school, then—"

"You are never going back to school!" Dad yells, making it clear that I have no say in any of this, that I've completely lost control over my own life.

Everything around me turns to a red blur as my eyes fill with tears. "Please, let's—"

"Just stop!" he shouts, the words echoing through the canyon over and over again.

I'm shaking now. I feel my anger growing out of control, and I know what I'm supposed to do when that happens—take a walk or a shower, do some yoga, write poetry, tie my figure eights, knead my balloon of flour. And I know what I'm *not* supposed to do.

I stare at him, heart pounding, hands trembling, eyes spilling. I don't want to take a walk or do some yoga. I want to fight and scream and cry and lash out. So I do. "I hate you."

His face fills with anguish before he turns away from me, picking up his backpack and latching it to his body, making it clear he's done with this discussion, which was hardly ever a discussion at all.

I'm not done. But when Dad whips around, his face stops me. The anger, the hurt has all drained out of it like the blood from his shot leg. His eyes widen. His mouth opens. All that's left is fear. Tremendous fear.

I don't understand.

Then I feel it.

The ground vibrates beneath our feet. Small pebbles and sheets of sand break free of cracks and crevices in the shuddering canyon walls. They tumble to the ground. It must be a stampede or an earthquake. But how could there be a stampede down here? And we don't have earthquakes in the desert. Not like this.

It's behind me. I'm terrified to look. But I need to know. I need to know what it is. And so I turn to face it.

My brain can barely understand what it's seeing, and so

    I

          send

                my

                        mind

                              to

                                    another

                                          place.

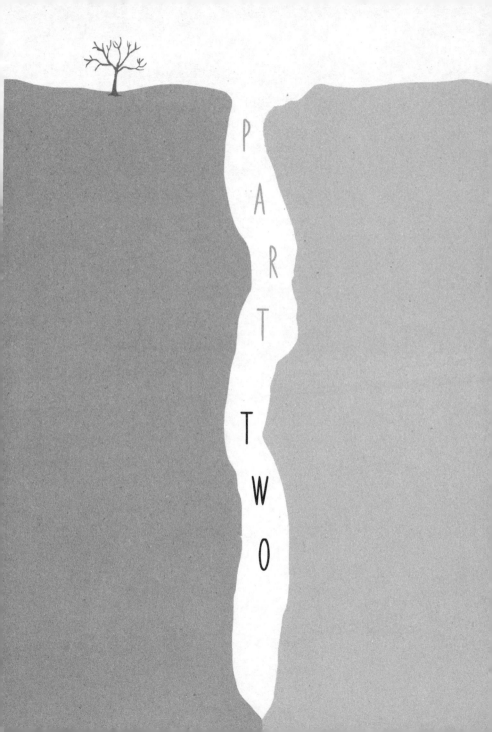

PART

TWO

BLACK WATER

An enormous wall
of black water
heads straight for us.

It carries
all the desert:
uprooted ironwoods,
ocotillo wands,
cholla balls,
animals,
rock,
mud,
and death.

EIGHT SECONDS

Eight seconds
> I am frozen again in fear.

Seven seconds
> Dad screams at me to climb.

Six seconds
> I reach for my backpack,
> but he grabs me,
> the strap slipping
> from my fingers.

Five seconds
> Dad throws me on top of the outcropping
> where I lay a few minutes ago.

Four
> I search for anything I can hang on to,
> a crack, a small indent in the wall,
> an embedded rock.

Three

Dad pulls himself on top of the outcropping
as I struggle to climb the wall.

Two

Dad pushes me up to where I find
a foothold above his head.

One

Dad grabs a crack in the wall
while I grip the same vertical crack above him
and brace myself.

HITTING

The water
    hits like a
        train
I grip
    the
        wall
    not wanting
    to fall
    and get crushed
    underneath its
        wheels
the water
    rises as quickly
    as the
        bile
    shooting
    up
    my
        throat

sweeps away
    my backpack
    and every supply
I look
  for more
    footholds
  climb higher
  and slip
  and
  nearly
  plunge
  down
  into
  the
  foaming
    water
I grip
  any
    hold
  I can find
  with my trembling
    fingers
  in my
    panic

to get away

from the

      water

splashing me

spraying in my

      mouth

covering my

      tongue

with its

      salt

more like the

      ocean

than a

      river

TOO

Dad clings to the crack
below me, the water
now flowing over his legs,
stronger than the force of gravity
moving in the wrong direction,
doing everything in its power
to break him free of the wall.

I look down at his
tense, red face,
clenched teeth,
white knuckles
straining to hold on.

He can't.
He doesn't have the strength.
I'm going to lose him

too.

THE LAST THING

I love you
> and
> *I'm sorry*
> and
> *Hold on*
>> are the last things
>> he says to me,
>> though I barely
>> hear the words
>>> over the
>>> screeching
>>> screaming
>>> in my mind
>>>> over the
>>>> roaring,
>>>> rushing
>>>> black water,

which finally
accomplishes its goal
of tearing him
from the wall.
            He's carried away,
            lying on his back,
            floating on his backpack,
            hands folded over his chest,
                    trying not to drown,
                    trying to flow with the water.
            I watch him
            until he disappears.
                    I didn't have time to say,
                    I love you, too.
                    The last thing
                    I said to my dad was

I hate you.

LIVING WATER

I've seen
rivers and ponds
form instantly
when the heavy monsoons
dump inches of water
on the desert in seconds.

I've seen flash floods before.
But I've never seen one
like this.

The waters

churn and turn
and roil and boil
and swirl and whorl
and foam and form
into dizzying whirlpools,
then dissolve.

I have to remind myself
the water's not alive;
it won't reach up
with slender, flowing fingers
and take me,

       pry me,

         snatch me,

from this wall,
suck me down
into its
violently whirling,
tirelessly turbulent
mouth.

The fear,
the anxiety,
controls me,
is in every part of me,
as I cling
to this wall of stone.

What do you fear, Eleanor?

Dying.

Are you likely to die in this situation?

Yes.

WAITING

The water arrived
like a tsunami,
but it leaves
like bathwater
trickling down
a hair-clogged drain.

I hug the wall,
every muscle
tense and aching,
my body
one big ball
of pain.

I wait
and wait
and wait
as the water slowly,
painfully lowers,
getting drunk

by the eternally
thirsty ground.

I will it to drink
faster before I fall.

I wait for
seconds,
     minutes,
          hours,
               days,
                    months,
                        years.

My muscles shake
with fatigue.
My vision blurs
with tears.
My heart pounds
with the full force
of having to watch
both my parents
torn apart.

SHAME

Self-condemnation
from unprocessed guilt and shame
is never helpful.

DAD'S HEIGHT

By the time the canyon is gray,
the water is finally low enough
for me to drop onto the outcropping.
I look down through a curtain of sweaty, damp hair,
already wishing I hadn't taken out my ponytail,
and see the rock, the waters just beneath it
now flowing at a stroll rather than a sprint.

It's about six feet down.
Dad's height.
Because that's how high he could lift me.
The pain and pressure in my chest grow
as if someone is punching my heart.

I have to climb down,
but I know before I even begin
it's impossible.
Climbing down is nothing
like climbing up.
Plus, I have boots on,
and the wall below me is wet.

I don't have any choice.
I can't hang on to this wall another minute,
and I don't have the strength to climb up
out of this canyon.

My heart pounds hard enough
to send tremors through my body,
make my fingers, hands, and arms shudder.
Lowering one unsteady boot
for a foothold below me,
I cry
because
I know
I'm about
to fall.

SLIPPING

My boot slips,
my fingers, hands, and arms
too weak to hang on.
Sliding down the wall,
slowing my fall with friction,
sanding skin off my
palms, forearms, and knees,
my body so filled with adrenaline,
I don't yet feel the pain.

I hit the outcropping,
boots first,
and my feet slip out from under me.
My right hip, ribs, arm slam
against the rocky ledge,
my teeth knocking together,
biting my tongue.

I slide into the water,
frantically grasp at the crack in the rock,
and stop myself,
half my body in the water,
which is trying to pull me from the ledge.

I drag myself out,
my mouth filling with blood,
lie on my side, and pull
my legs up to my chest.

And now the pain comes.
It radiates
over my torn skin
like a fire,
barrels into my battered bones
like a fighter.
Blood drips
from my hands and knees and mouth
onto the rock.
It spreads like watercolors
on the wet stone.

THE SECOND TIME

I've lost my
backpack,
hoodie,
hair tie,
helmet,
harness,
gloves,
food,
water,
last person in my life.

I have nothing left.
Except my life.

That's the second time in a single year
one of my parents put my life
before theirs.

SINKING

The canyon is dimming.
I need to get moving
before it gets too dark.
I need to find Dad.

It's risky to walk in the desert
with no light at all.
There could be
snakes, scorpions, spiny cactuses.

I push myself up,
my arms shaking with the effort,
still worn out from clinging to the wall.

I lean over and look down
at the ground a few feet below,
puddles everywhere but no longer
enough water to flow.

I drag my legs around
and shove myself off the rock.
My boots sink deep into the dark
sludge like quicksand.

Too deep.

I'm stuck.
Stuck in this muck,
my muscles too fatigued
to pull out my boot.

I grasp my leg with both hands
and pull with all my strength.
My boot finally breaks free
with a loud sucking sound,
completely soaked in sludge.

I won't be walking anywhere tonight,
so I climb back up on the rock.

Maybe Dad didn't go too far.
I cry out for him,
hoping he'll hear,
hoping he'll call back.
I listen.

Nothing.

I'll have to wait here
on this rock for now.
Just for now until Dad returns.

WHY?

I lie back on the rock
and watch as the silver sliver of sky
above me turns to black,
taking all light in the canyon with it.

There's nothing to do
except let my mind wander
to places I don't want to visit.

It's always the same places.
Even here and now.

Why, why, why?

There has to be a reason why a person
would walk into a restaurant

and   just   start   shooting.

I need to know the reason so desperately
that Dad sent me to Mary.

But Mary still hasn't told me why.

And if there's no why,
then I'm just small and powerless,

a single drop of water
in a raging river,
a single grain of sand
in a suffocating dust storm,
a single speck of palo verde pollen
floating on the dry desert breeze.

Unanchored.
Untethered.
Unpredictable.

Unable to see
what the future holds.

Unable to see
where I'll land.

ONE RAGING RIVER

I badly need to know why right now. But no one is here to tell
me why, so I imagine it for myself. I remember those dark
mountains to the west. I picture rain running down the
sides of the mountains in hundreds of small streams,
which become tens of brooks, which become
a few creeks, which become one raging
river in a previously dry riverbed
that gradually deepens into
a narrow slot canyon.
One raging river
that washes
my father
away.

WHAT IF?

As though my mind
is made of metal,
it's pulled by a magnet
to another place,
an *unhelpful, unhealthy* place.
It's the place of what–ifs.

What if
I'd picked another restaurant?

What if
we'd sat at a different table?

What if
we'd gone for lunch instead of dinner?

What if
it wasn't my birthday?

Then Mom would still be here.
Dad would still be here.

And I wouldn't be here
alone
at the bottom of a dark canyon.

BREATHING

And so I am sitting on this
cold, wet rock in the dark
alone with my thoughts,
with the　　　whys
and the　　　what-ifs.

And I feel myself
falling deeper and deeper
into my anger, which spirals
like the brightening stars above me.

It's a tornado turning,
a choppy sea churning,
a bone-dry desert burning
evermore out of control.

My heart pounds.
I want to scream.

Remember your breathing, Eleanor.

I cry out for Dad again,
funneling my anger, my breath,
into my voice.

My cries echo over and over
against the tall canyon walls,
following the path of the flood.
The path to Dad.

BUT

Dad's a great swimmer,   but his leg.

Dad's strong,   but those floodwaters
may be stronger.

Dad has his backpack,   but all that debris,
the water so filled
with sticks and stones
and sludge,
could tear it from
his body.

Dad knows how
to survive in the desert,   but he's never faced
anything like this.

I know he's out there
somewhere in the dark
of this canyon,   but is he still alive?

Yes.
He's alive and he
knows where I am.
He'll find me,   but I know he can't
                                  find me tonight
                                  in the dark and the mud.

I lie back on the cold rock,
a trill floating back to me
from somewhere
down the canyon.

DAD!

TRILL

I sit up.
Listen.
It sounds like a whistle.
Dad is whistling for me.

Wait.
Did Dad bring a whistle?

The trill rings
through the canyon
again and again.
And then something
is trilling very close to me.
And then several somethings
are trilling all around me
like a screeching chorus.

Folding my legs up,
I press my forehead into my knees,
push my hands back through my hair,
and squeeze it tightly at my scalp.

It's not Dad.

It's the red–spotted toads,
digging themselves out
from under the soaked ground.

I lie down on my side
and clamp my hands over my ears
to try to block them out.

WIND

I know it must be at least midnight
because the toads finally quiet back down.
I lift my hands from my ears
and rub them over my chilled arms.

I remember camping with Mom and Dad
at the bottom of Canyon de Chelly,
how the winds blew at night.
I can still hear them
groaning against our tent walls.
The sound, almost deafening,
frightened me.

I thought it was monsters.

It's just the wind, Nora,
Dad assured me, hugging me to him.
When the canyon walls cool at night
it causes the air to blow hard.
Don't worry, sweetheart.
Nothing can hurt us down here.

The next morning our Diné guide told us,
The winds are part of the way
the canyon expresses siihasin,
harmony.

But all I feel right now is
disharmony.

Our Diné guide told us,
The canyon gives much to those
who would receive it.

That may be true of Canyon de Chelly,
but I don't think this canyon
has anything to give me.

This canyon only takes away.

BURNING

The canyon winds pick up
and slice over me like an icicle.
My body starts
to shake uncontrollably.
My clothes are still damp,
and the wind is like winter.

For the 366th night in a row,
I wish my mom were here
to take me in her arms
and comfort me
and sing the song
she used to sing.

But she's not.

So my mind goes back
to the last time
I saw her alive,
how she wished me
Happy birthday, sweetheart,
and the guitarist played a song
while I ate fried ice cream
with a bright blue candle
burning.

FLAME

Another mom was there.

Sofía Moreno,
just a regular mom,
sitting in the booth next to ours.

I remember how she and her two little boys
had clapped when the server
brought out their fajitas,
how she'd pulled her kids to her
to keep them from touching
the flame.

And so my thoughts keep
circling back to
fire.

DRIFTING

With nothing but
whys and what-ifs
and burning memories
and freezing winds
to keep me company,
my eyes start to feel as heavy
as the boulders the flood
washed away like pebbles.

How
     can I
          possibly sleep
               when I'm so cold?

How

    can I

        possibly sleep?

How

    can I?

How...

NIGHTMARE

First come the tremendous
booms.

My mother, singing to me seconds ago,
is shoving me under the table
so frantically, so desperately,
that I bash my head on the edge
and her fingers leave bruises on my body.

What   *is*   *happening?*

Then more
booms
    and Mom is covered in
blood.

Dad is screaming, screaming, screaming,
    and there are more
booms
    and more
blood.

I squeeze my eyes shut
as I press my cheek to Mom's knee,
then I force my eyes open
and turn my head, smearing her blood
across my face.

I see his lower half
from under the table:
enormous camouflaged
legs and boots.
I see the tip of his weapon and then him,
slowly, gradually, deliberately
bending over to find me
under the table.

I am frozen,
can't move,
can't scream,
can't breathe,
can't think anything but

I   am   going   to   die.

This time he'll get to me
before the
blur of brown legs.
Sofía Moreno's legs.

When she did what she did.

REBUILD

The yipping of coyotes above
startles me awake on this hard rock,
my body filled with tremors,
every nerve shooting pain.

I know I shouldn't.
I know I'm not supposed to,
but I won't let him near me.

So I build my wall,
and I lay

my	shame
and	brick
and	anger
and	stone
and	guilt
and	clay
and	fear
and	rock
and	hate.

Layer after layer,
but I know, deep inside,
it's really all just
Frosted Flakes.

WEAKNESS

I wait for numbness.
I am colder than I've ever been,
both   inside   and   out.

The wall won't hold, Eleanor.

Yes   it   will.

Rewrite your nightmare.

Don't   make   me
think   about   him.

*Rewrite it into something where you
are stronger, braver, more powerful.*

But   I'm   not.

But you are.

ALMOST

~~I am freezing.~~
I am almost freezing.
If I were frozen,
I would be numb, peaceful,
asleep, but not dreaming.
In some horrible way,
I wish I were completely frozen
because that wouldn't hurt
as much as almost,
because I wouldn't have to feel
him clawing at every tiny gap in my wall
that is almost strong enough
to keep him out.

LIE

Who is the Beast, Eleanor?

The Beast
Only exists in my dreams.
Really, he's just
Make-believe,
Everything about him
Nonexistent.
The Beast isn't rational
Or
Real.

NOT REAL

I feel lost, floating
in the ink of the canyon.

I slip in and out of consciousness,
too exhausted to stay awake,
too cold to fully sleep.

I curl my body
into a tight ball,
hug my legs
to my chest,
rub my bare arms,
breathe warmth
into my sore, sanded hands.

I wonder how much my body
temperature
is
dropping,
and I curse myself
for taking off my hoodie.

This night will never end.

Every time I drift, I hear him coming
closer,
closer;
every time I feel my mind slip away
before startling awake again.

Drifting,
waking,
drifting,
waking
all night long.

Shivering,
shuddering,
shaking,
quaking
    all night long.

Telling myself
he's not real,
he's not real,
he's not real,
    all night long.

But
never
ever
rewriting anything
    all night long.

WONDER

And then, something wondrous:

The sky is lighting again.
Relief at seeing the light
fills me up, spills over,
down my cheeks
and onto the cold rock.

I watch the sun turn
the ribbon of sky above me
from speckled black velvet
to deep purple satin
to beautiful pink silk.

I've made it through the torturous night.
My wall held.
I kept him away.

STAY

I need to move, to heat my cold body.
Pushing myself up, I peer at the ground,
which still looks damp.
I carefully slide down the rock,
allowing one boot to touch the ground.
It doesn't sink in nearly as much as last night,
so I put both feet down.
My legs give out, and I stumble,
my knees digging into the soaked silt,
mud smothering and sanding and stinging my sores.
I stand up, dizzy, spinning, leaning
against the outcropping.

I focus on putting one foot in front of the other,
concentrate on taking step after step.
My rubbery legs feel more steady with each movement.
My breathing evens out. My heart slows its slamming.

I stop.
Should I instead walk to the Jeep?
Break a window? Wait for help? Who would come?

Too hot, no water, all supplies swept away.

Walk to the main road?
How far is it? Could I find the way?

Too hot, no water, all supplies swept away.

I look down the canyon in the direction of Dad
making his way back to me right now
I know.

He would never leave without me,
and I won't leave without him.

COLORS

I find a small puddle in a hollow spot on a rock
and lap up as much water as I can.
Then I look up at the slice of sky
and long to be in the sun again.

The canyon looks different today.

Lychen bursts like fireworks around me
in different shades of green:
lime and split pea and mint.
The layers wobble and waver.
It's as though a small child
ran through the canyon
while I lay on the rock all night
and colored the walls
outside the lines with
wild scribbles in
deep, angry red crayon.

STEPS

I focus on taking one step at a time
toward Dad.
He'll find me.
He's walking back to me right now,
just as I'm walking to him.
Then we'll figure it all out together.

Step, step, step.

The air is warming.
My steps are faster.
My body is heating.
I'm so thirsty.
I stop at every puddle I find
in the sunken spots on rocks.
Each one seems smaller than the last.

I climb over a large boulder
blocking the narrow path
then reach a broader opening,
grateful for the space,
wide enough to let in more light,
wide enough for a flood-tattered ironwood tree,
debris littering its broken branches,
to grow from a seed blown down a long time ago.

Step, step, step.

I move around the tree
and the canyon narrows again,
shuts out the light.

Step, step, step.

Dad will find me soon.

LOSS

I see something in the distance,
sticking out of the ground.
As I near it, I find
a piece of garbage,
washed into the canyon
from who knows where.

An old plastic cup.
A sign of human life.
Garbage.

But a cup can be useful.
A cup can hold water.

Lifting it out of the mud, I find it's only
part of a cup.

I try to put it in my pocket,
but it crumbles,
brittle from the brutal heat.

I wipe the pieces from my sore palms,
and they flutter to the ground
around a pile of broken shale.

One shard of gray shale catches my eye,
and I pick it up.
It's flat and sharp on one end.
I run a finger along the razor-like edge.
It scratches me, draws a tiny amount of blood.

I slip the rock into my back pocket.
This stone knife could be useful
down here in the canyon.

I imagine myself using it
to skin the hide from a kangaroo rat
and snort at the thought.

I move my hand to my front pocket,
but the heart-shaped stone isn't there.
My eyes blur and my lip quivers
and I want to crumble to the ground
like the fluttering, brittle bits of broken cup.

I wipe my eyes and bite my lip
and stay standing.
I don't have time to get all
bent out of shape over a lost rock.

ENDLESS WALLS

The light
lowers
down the wall,
warming
the canyon.

How long have I been walking?
It's hard to tell when I can't
see the sun.
It already feels like I've walked
      inches,
            feet,
                  yards,
                        miles,
                            and
                                miles.

My steps quicken
and my heart speeds with anticipation
as I round every new corner,
expecting Dad to appear.

But all I find are more
walls made of waves,
like the water that carved them.

DEADLY

That sound. Effervescent.
Sizzling. Like Dad frying
sausage in the morning.

Coiled. Head held high and back.
Ready to spring, fill me with venom
if I get too near.

Tongue flicks over and over again,
smelling me, figuring me out.

A narrow tunnel of sunlight shines down
into the canyon, cracking the silt
under my feet and warming the snake.

It's also drying the last of my puddles
and scorching my pale, sun-starved skin.
It must be about noon.

I pick up a stone from the canyon floor
and toss it at the snake,
which rattles its warning at me.

But it doesn't move.

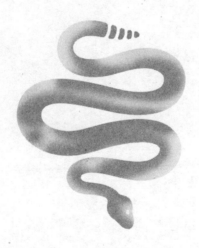

AWAY

I am so, so tired.
I am swaying on my feet.
I sit down on a rock
out of striking distance
and study the snake.

Looks like a diamondback
but
greenish tinge,
fading diamond pattern,
white rings on tail
wider than black rings.

It's a Mojave.
Deadly venomous.
I have no choice
but to wait it out.

My head nods in exhaustion.
The warmth is like a drug,
dragging me under.

I keep my boots
on the canyon floor
as I lean to the side
and rest my head on the rock.
The stone is warm against my cheek
and arms, and I am instantly
drifting,
no longer concerned
about the deadly snake in my way.

I am gone, floating away,
into the darkness of my mind,
away to the place where he can find me.

ANOTHER LIE

You can be honest, Eleanor.
Who is the Beast?

Maybe you're not listening,
Or don't want to listen, but I have
No more to
Say.
The Beast is not
Even
Real.

PANIC

Booms
    always come first.
    Then the
blood.

I hear him.
He's catching up with me.

Crunch.
Crunch.
Crunch.

I startle awake.
Jump off the rock,
then stumble back,
away from the rattling snake
I'd so quickly forgotten.

    Do it now, Eleanor.
    Rewrite your nightmare.

I can't.
I am spiraling,
untethered and wild,
like the whirlpools
I spied in the flood.

I am sure the Beast is coming,
and the rattling of the snake
has become chains,
and the red of the canyon
has become blood,
and the shadows of the canyon
have become death.

Ground yourself, Eleanor.

COPING

Grounding techniques for
coping with PTSD:
Use your five senses.

GROUNDING

Where am I?
In the canyon.

What do I see?
The snake, walls around me,
dirt below me.

What do I hear?
The rattling.
At home I'd turn on music,
but here I speak out loud.
I am here, in the canyon.

What do I feel?
I reach out and touch
the canyon wall:
rough, warm stone.
I bend down and grab
a handful of dirt,
massage it
between my hands.

What do I smell?
The desert:
creosote, sage, and dust.

What do I taste?
At home, I keep
a jar of chocolates
in my room.
I put one in my mouth
and focus on the melting
to keep me grounded
in the here and now.
In the canyon,
I taste only the bitterness
of my unbrushed mouth.

Who is with me?
No one but this snake.
No one but this snake.
No one but this snake.

Are you likely to die in this situation?

Yes.

KEEP MOVING

     Move!
I yell at the snake.
     Move, move, move!

But it only rattles back at me.

I need to keep moving,
so I don't fall back asleep,
so I can find Dad.

     Move, move, move!

But it will be me
who will have to move.

And so I run
around the snake,
but
too quickly,
too carelessly,
too clumsily.

It strikes
at my ankles.
I jump,
stumble,
crawl,
just out
of its reach.

It is poised
for another strike
as I back away
like a crab,
then scramble
to my feet
and run away.

NEEDLES

My run-in with the snake has left me
shaky, sweaty, dry-mouthed.
I need water,
but my precious puddles are gone.

I spot a barrel cactus
growing low enough for me to reach,
run to it, study it,
but I'm not sure what species it is.

Dad taught me there's
only one kind
that won't make me violently sick.

I pull out my sharp shale,
attempt to pierce the cactus,
but instead, the needles pierce me.
I try to shave the needles off,
but they don't give.
Raising my foot high, I kick at them.
One needle pierces my boot,
buries itself in my heel.

Stumbling back on my butt,
I cry out in pain,
then dig the needle out of my shoe.

Standing again, I stare down the cactus.
Did I really think I could open
this tough, unyielding thing
with only my stone knife?

My eyes well with tears,
but I wipe them away.
Really, it's for the best.
I'm not sure what species it is,
and that's a mistake I shouldn't make.

DIGGING

I have no other choice
but to fall back to the ground,
my knees in the mud,
which already isn't as wet
as it was this morning.

I
push
my
hands
into
the
cool
ground.

I dig down deep,
throwing the wet dirt to the side.

My long hair falls in my face,
and I push my muddy hands through it
over and over to keep it back.
Why did I have to undo my ponytail?

My fingernails are dark with mud,
and I hear Mom's voice.
> *Are you growing watermelons in there?*
> *Save one for me, please.*

Mom loved watermelon.

I think of Danielle
as I dig and dig and dig.

When we tried mud masks
and got mud all over the bathroom,
door handles, couch, and carpet.

How we'd each written a word
on each other's foreheads,
and then couldn't stop laughing
when we looked in the mirror and saw
we'd both spelled out the same thing:
POOP.

Dad said we shared
the same strange brain.
But if that were true,
we'd still be friends.

I dig and I dig and I swipe
hair from my face
with muddy hands, and I wait,
but the water doesn't pool.

I fall back and stare at my stupid hole,
the mud tossed around the edges.
Breathing hard, sweating.
Hair blanketing my face.
My heel still throbbing from the cactus needle.

It's always harder than I expect.

BEFORE AND AFTER

I sit and think and breathe
and twist one long strand
of hair around my finger.

I hold the strand in front of my face
and stare at the clear line of my
Before and After hair,
where my life broke
into two parts,
so easily identifiable,
like a ring in a tree thinner than the rest,
indicating a drought occurred that year
in the high desert, forcing the people
to move on to another place.

A park ranger taught us that at Montezuma Castle,
when the three of us used to adventure.

The foot of hair from the tip
is my Before hair.
It's streaked with gold, red, brown, and blond,
as though it's reflecting
the colors of the canyon,
vivid and shining and alive,
grown during a time
of safety, love, and adventure.

My Before hair is
hair my mother would have touched
when she was asking me about my school day
or telling me a new story idea.

My Before hair is
hair Danielle would have braided into a fishtail
while we watched movies in the middle of the night,
hair she would have rubbed lemon into
before we lay out by the pool together.

My Before hair is
hair that would have been
regularly washed, brushed, and styled.

The six inches of hair from the root
is my After hair.

My After hair is
irregularly washed, brushed, and never styled,
except to be put up in a ponytail.

My After hair is
only one shade, having been kept in the dark,
unchanged by desert days
filled with chlorine and sun and adventure.

My After hair has never been touched
by Mom or Danielle.

How can I do this?
How can I make it
through the canyon
with all of this Before and After
in my face the entire way?

A DRINK

An idea finally comes.
I need to separate
sand and water.

Filter. Strain.

I remove my white tank top
and lay it on the ground.
I scoop handfuls of mud onto my shirt,
fold it up like a sack,
and hold it over my head,
opening my mouth widely,
my chapped lips tight and stinging.
I squeeze.

It's quiet in the canyon,
except for the buzzing of a fly
that has found me.
It whirs around my tossed-back head,
making me feel even dizzier
while brown water trickles into my mouth.

I don't have anything better
than this dirty tank top to filter it.
No iodine tablets to purify it.
No fire to boil it.
But I'll be out of here
before sickness has time to set in.

CARRIED AWAY

The short amount of direct sunlight
has already burned my white shoulders.
I take some mud and slather it on my
stinging skin, dab it under my eyes
before moving on.

Keeping track of the time is difficult
when I can't see the sun.
The line of sunlight along one canyon wall
is now rising.

Three o'clock?
Four o'clock?

Where is Dad?
How can we not have
found each other by now?
I feel as if I've walked
a hundred miles.

And then I see color ahead,
coiled in an uprooted palo verde
like a bright red snake.
As I near it, my heart leaps.
I throw my hands up to my muddy face
and laugh out loud
before skipping the last few steps to the tree.

The limbs
scratch and slice,
mar and mangle,
injure and inflame
my arms and legs.

Its slender, green branches
snap and slash,
lick and lash,
whip and welt
my face.

Its thorny claws
clasp and catch,
tug and tear,
rip and rend
my long hair.

I hardly feel any of it.
All I feel is my heart pounding in excitement
as I continue unraveling the rope
from the tree that carried it away.

It's probably taken me over an hour
to get the rope free, my arms and legs
now as layered in shades of red
as the canyon walls,
my long strands of hair
fluttering in the branches,
my face stinging with scrapes.

But I don't care.
I couldn't leave it behind.
This rope might mean so much to us.

PATTERNS

Apophenia:
trying to find a pattern
when there isn't one.

SEARCHING

You enjoy poetry. Right, Eleanor?

I like my mom's poetry.

Have you heard of Gerard Manley Hopkins?

No.

He was a poet who would sit on a cliff
and sketch sea waves, wave after wave after wave,
to see whether one ever repeated.

Why?

He was searching for a pattern.
He believed if he sketched the same wave twice,
it would be proof.

Proof of what?

That there really was a god.
Perhaps that's why we have such a need
to find patterns, a reason for everything.
Do you think you're searching for a pattern?

Always.

And so I watch the canyon walls as I walk.
Waves made of
          sand and stone
instead of
          salt water.

I look down at the ground,
at looser gray sand running in waves
over the crackled, light pink silt.

Looking for patterns in the waves
of the ground.
Looking for patterns in the waves
of the walls.

I'm searching for repeats, reproductions, replicas.
And I know if I find one, it will comfort me.
It will mean this is all happening for a reason.
This has all been designed by a designer.

But my vision is blurry and my mind is fuzzy.
I can't make out the details in the walls or ground,
especially when the light in the canyon
begins to dim.

DRYING

I fall back to the ground
and push my fingers in,
but the ground hardly gives.
I pull the sharp shale from my pocket
and plunge it into the earth,
grasping the rock with both hands,
trying to shovel the dirt
out of the hardening soil.

I remove my tank top again,
scoop small mounds of damp dirt into it.
Once more, I fold it up
and squeeze it over my mouth,
longing for another drizzle of dirty water.

But all I get this time is drops.

STILL

I still haven't found Dad.
Dad still hasn't found me.
He must have been carried
very far, but we have to be,
we *have* to be,
much closer to finding each other.

I cry out for him once more.
Maybe he can hear me now.
But all that comes back
is the echo of my own voice.

What if
he's not coming?

What if
he's badly hurt?

What if
he's unconscious?

What if
he's—

> *Focusing on what-ifs*
> *helps nothing, Eleanor.*

PROTECTION

Searching around boulders
and scanning the canyon walls
for any kind of inlet,
I look for a place, a hidden place,
that will guard me from the night winds.

Down here in the canyon,
I am completely hidden, and yet,
it seems there's nowhere to hide.

I finally find a large boulder
with a good-sized outcropping.
I bend down and peek under it,
hoping it's big enough to tuck myself
into its safety.
It is, but my head drops,
my heart sinks, my shoulders slump.

It's filled with thorny twigs,
and more important,
cholla balls buried in the mud.
Someone was already living
under this rock before it got destroyed:
a pack rat.

Like the cactus wren, the pack rat
uses the vicious spines of the cholla
to protect itself.
I think of the cactus wren
and her constant, quick
ah, ah, ah, ah, ah, ah.
I think of her nest, surrounded by,
supported by, the arms of the cholla.
She uses pain as protection.

I guess I can understand,
but no human being could bear to sleep
in a bed of cholla.

ONE CALORIE

I find another hidden place and peer inside.
It's too small for me, but...

Yes! Thank you.

I reach inside and pull out
the mesquite beans,
a couple slipping through my jittery fingers
and falling to the canyon floor.
I've stumbled upon an animal's hoard,
something to eat, to ease the cramping
in my empty stomach.

I don't care how old they are.
I don't care how dirty they are.

I   am   starving.

I shake the pods
so I can hear the stone-hard seeds,

small and shaped like a sunflower's.
They rattle like the snake,
so I know the pods are ready to eat.

I shove one slender bean in my mouth
and bite down, snapping the pod in half,
then chewing, trying to get to the edible
part of the pod, the pulp, the pith.

As woody as a stick,
sweet like syrup gone bad, sucking
every calorie I can before spitting
out the hard seeds and sawdust,
which coats all of my sore tongue
and sticks between every tooth.
Spitting so much out that I wonder
whether any is sinking into my stomach.

One calorie.
Maybe two.
But one is better than none.

I shove the few remaining
pods in my pockets
to save for later.

DIMMING

The sky continues to dim.
Soon it will be dark again,
and I still haven't found shelter.
I still haven't found Dad.

Then I hear the booms
and freeze in fear.

More storms. More water.
I can't sleep on the canyon floor.

I pick up as much speed as I can,
jogging and stumbling,
panting and dizzy,
trying to beat
the fading light.

It might happen again.

Dad's face filled with terror.

There won't be any moonlight.

My body frozen in fear.

I won't see the ground to run away.

Tremors beneath our feet.

I won't see the walls to climb them.

Shuddering all around us.

I will hear it.

Roaring like a train.

I will feel it.

Trembling like an earthquake.

But I won't see it coming.

Enormous wall of water.

ANXIETY

Flash.   Boom!

My breathing speeds
out of control
as my anxiety
rises as high
as the towering walls
of the canyon,
growing grayer
with
every
       passing
           minute.

Flash.   Boom!

And then I stop,
trying to catch my breath,
throwing my head back,
gasping for air.

There.
I see it.
A place
large enough for me
in the canyon wall.

Could something be living in there?
I squint, focus my eyes, don't see anything
but those white drips Dad pointed out.
Bats.
If any have tucked themselves in the corners,
I'll scare them away.

Flash.   Boom!

But the fluttering in my stomach and heart
doesn't stop.

Flash.   Boom!

Because this refuge
is about twenty feet up.

FREE SOLO

Eleanor, do you ever feel reckless?

As the canyon walls cool, and the distant booms
become louder, the wind picks up
and brushes my chilled arms.

No, I'm very careful.
I know now how easily I can die.

I study the cave, spot a rock jutting out
near the opening I can tie the rope around
to lower myself back down later.

You don't ever feel like you're invincible?

I remove my boots and socks,
tying the boot laces together
and slinging them over my shoulder,
the socks stuffed inside.

Not really. Sometimes it just feels
like I don't care. So yeah, maybe that's reckless.

I tie the rope in a loop and wear it across
my chest like a cross-shoulder bag.

You don't care? About what?

I've never climbed
without rope,
without rock shoes,
without chalk,
without a harness,
without a belayer
standing at the bottom,
taking up my slack
and keeping me safe
so I don't plummet to the earth.

About...me. About my life.

This will be the first wall I've ever climbed
with nothing but myself,
with my hair in my face the whole way to the top.

Sometimes I feel like I don't care at all.
Like none of it matters.
Like my life doesn't matter.

I know I could die if I fall.

But usually I'm very cautious.

Break a leg, and I'll be left to drown.

I never really feel…

But I don't think I'll live anyway
if I stay down here one more night.

In-between.

TERRIFIED

I braid my tangled hair
and hope it will stay back.

I bend down and rub
dirt between my hands
since I have no chalk.

Running my bare feet over the dirt,
I scan the wall under the cave,
looking for any cracks
I can slip my fingers into.
Just a small crack will do.

My hair is already
breaking free of its braid.

I work out the ascent in my mind,
squinting in the deepening twilight,
following a path
from the ground to the cave.

Slipping my fingers into a crack
and finding a small foothold,
I pull myself up.
Good.

One step at a time, Eleanor.

I find another foothold and move
one hand above the other in the crack.

My parents lived for this
when they were both living.

Right now, more than ever,
I wish I had Dad's skill,
Mom's passion.

They met on the face
of a thousand-foot-tall cliff.

They spent their honeymoon
zip-lining over rainforests.

They rafted the whitewater
of the Colorado.

They paraglided off mountains
and into canyons.

They strapped me to their backs
when I was an infant and hiked
the Grand Canyon.

They taught me everything they knew
about the desert, hoping I would one day
love it as much as they did.

My parents
rappelled, climbed, hiked
in this desert.

And so I never wanted
to disappoint them by telling them
I'm terrified of heights.

FALLING

Looking down for another foothold,
my hair falls forward
over my eyes.

I blow at it,
but it flops right back.

I can't see.
I can't see another foothold.

I release one of my hands
and push my hair back,
but as soon as I look down
for another foothold,
it falls in my face.
I tuck it behind my ears
as securely as I can.

I move my foot to a small
foothold and settle it firmly.
But when I lift my other leg,
I slip.

The rough wall
tears my skin,
peels fresh layers
off my arms and knees and shins.

The ground knocks
the wind out of my lungs,
and I claw at my chest,
trying to find the air,
my whole body
stinging with scrapes
and scratches and tears.

NO ONE

I braid my hair again.
Once more I find the footholds,
going faster,
keeping my body close to the wall
to save my energy,
using my legs more than my arms.

One step at a time, Eleanor.

Soon, I'm ten feet above the ground.
Thunder booms loud enough to rattle
my teeth, my insides, my fingers.
They tremble as I look down
for a new foothold.

My hair breaks free,
falls in my face,
my stomach lurching
from both seeing
and then not being able to see.

My body is shaking,
my breaths coming too fast and hard.
I might vomit.
This was a mistake, a horrible mistake.
What was I thinking?
I can't do this.
I need to get back down.

Pushing my hair behind my ears,
I look for a way down,
even though I know
there is none.
I slipped yesterday
after the flood because

no   one   climbs   down.

YOU CAN

I'm shivering and sweating,
losing all the water
I've drunk, and worse,
my fingers will get slippery.
A flash of light, and I wait
for the boom to rattle me
right off this wall.

You can do it, Eleanor.

I'm going to fall!

Self-efficacy, Eleanor.
Stop telling yourself you can't succeed.

The boom comes and goes
but doesn't knock me from the rock.
I look up and find a handhold.

One step at a time.

A few more movements,
and I'm finally able to reach one arm up,
grip the edge of the cave
as the rock beneath my foot
breaks away,
plummets
to the canyon floor.
My body slams
against the rough wall,
all breath
leaving my body
in a terrified whimper.

I dangle.

Are you likely to die in this situation?

Yes.

CAVE

I kick and flail
and stub toes
and tear toenails
and shred heels,
trying desperately
to hang on
to the wall.

> *Breathe, Eleanor.*
> *You're almost there.*

I peer through my hair
for a foothold,
my arms shaking
to hold my full weight.

I find one.

I settle my bare foot firmly
and pull myself up,
grunting,
growling,
teeth grinding
with the effort.

I crawl the few feet
across the small cave
and lean back against
a bumpy wall of stone,
waiting for my heart
and breathing to calm,
grateful I mostly used my legs
for the climb instead of my arms.
They wouldn't have held otherwise.

I toss my rope and boots on the floor.
It's cool in here, but the icy canyon winds
won't freeze my shredded skin,
and raging floodwaters can't reach me.

I hope they can't reach Dad, either,
wherever he is.

ANGER

Watch your anger cues:
heart racing, body shaking,
breath out of control.

RAGE

My head topples forward,
and my hair once more
falls in my face.

I breathe so hard that my hair
rises and falls,
rises and falls,
with my hyperventilating.
I pull the razor-sharp chunk of shale
from my pocket.

> *Make sure you're being kind to yourself, Eleanor,*
> *no matter how angry you feel.*

I press one finger
to the edge until it stings
before grasping several long strands.
I rub the sharp stone against my hair
until it tears apart,

gripping the sharp shale
with so much force
that it cuts into my hands
and blood drips
onto the floor of the cave.

Make sure you're being kind to your body.

I work at
hacking,
tearing,
ripping,
sawing
my hair out,
piece by piece.

Never, ever harm yourself.

It takes forever with the rock.
It tears the roots out of my scalp,
leaving my hair jagged.

Pay attention to your anger cues.

But I won't leave a single piece of hair
that can fall in my face
ever   again.

What can you do to manage that anger?

My teeth clench and my body vibrates
and my heart races with rage as I
hack,
tear,
rip,
saw
my hair out.

Relax your body.

When I'm done, I feel the cave floor
covered in my hair, and my hands
covered in blood, and my head
covered in an uneven, torn
mop of only
After hair.

Remember your deep breathing.

My rage overflows
as I throw the brittle chunk of slate
against the cave wall,
and it shatters into pieces.

SCREAMING

And I scream
    and scream
        and scream.

And my screams
fill
    the cave, and they
    spill
        over the side, blending into the
        trill
            of the red-spotted toads and into the
            shrill
                of the cold, windy canyon,
                and the winds carry
                my screams away.

I'm screaming out
the last of my water,
but I can't stop.

I scream until my chapped lips
are stretched so thin
the cracks open and bleed
into my mouth.

I scream until my voice
crackles and breaks and then is gone.

I reach out and swipe the hair
away from my body,
scatter the hair
across the cave floor,
push it frantically over the side.
When lightning flashes, I see
my bloodied hands have left
dark streaks across the stone.

The hair slides over the edge
of the cave into the canyon
to be carried away by the winds
along with my screams.

GONE

Collapsing against the wall of the cave,
I drop my face into my bloodied hands.

      My energy is
gone.
      My voice is
gone.
      My Before hair is
gone,
      along with all of my Before.

FEELING

Being alive means
sorrow, joy, pain, love, anger.
Feeling all the things.

NUMB

I pull my legs up to my chest
and gently rock,
my feet pressed to the cave floor,
the bumpy wall digging
into my back with the movement.

I focus on securing my wall.
I shove muddy
globs in the holes.
I stuff bloody
rags in the cracks.
I smear reeking
black tar over the surface
so nothing can get through.

    Don't build your wall, Eleanor.

This is too painful. I need it.

No, you don't.
It will only make you numb.

Numb sounds nice.

It's not.
You won't just be numb to pain,
but numb to joy, numb to compassion,
numb to love.

Living means feeling.
Tell me, Eleanor,

do you want to be dead?

No.

Because no longer feeling means
you are dead.

PIERCING

A sharp pinch in my back
pierces my numbness,
shows me I'm still alive.

It feels as though someone
has stabbed me
with a saguaro needle.
I let go of my knees
and grasp frantically at my back.

And now something is
crawling,
creeping
on my skin.

I let out a soundless shriek,
jump up and hit my head
on the low ceiling.

Another sharp pinch.
I've been stung twice.
By what I don't know.

Dizzy from the blow
to my head,
I struggle to peel off
my tank top
in the small space,
then throw it in the corner of the cave
away from me.

I grab my boots and strike and slap and slam them
against my shirt in the flickering light,
trying to kill whatever might be inside.

When lightning strikes,
I see the scorpion crawling out
and smash it again with my boots.
I try to make out what kind it is
in the flashing light.

The small size and shape
tell me all I need to know.

STUNG

I have been stung
by a bark scorpion,
the most venomous
scorpion in the desert.
Twice.

My thirsty veins
desperately lap up
every drop of venom.

My back begins to burn.
The flame spreads
like ripples over my skin.

Someone has taken a
blowtorch to my outsides
and filled my insides with ice.

My head
spins.
My tongue
swells.
My muscles
twitch.
My eyes
roll.
My insides
roil.

I lie on my side,
pull my legs up to my bare chest,
and concentrate on not vomiting
what muddy water I might have left
in my stomach.

HEART

I've never realized
how fast, loud, painful a heart
is able to beat.

REMEMBER

I pray for help,
though I don't know
who or what
could possibly help me
here inside a hole
in a wall
on the side of a canyon.

How long would it take
for someone to find my body?

Will anyone care?
Will they remember?

If I die here,
will people remember
Café Ardiente?

Will they remember
me, Dad, Mom?

Will they remember
Sofía Moreno,
just a regular mom
with two little boys
in the booth next to ours?

Because of what she did,
maybe I can find the fight
to keep going.

But I feel like I'm fading away,
and I don't have the strength
to stop it.

INSIDE A TENT

It's storming outside, light flashing
through the thin fabric.
I'm facing a wall—a tent wall.

I roll over and find Danielle
bundled in a sleeping bag,
big brown eyes watching me,
blankets pulled up to her nose,
face crinkled so I know
she's smiling.

What?

>   *I can't believe you*
>   *threw my fish back.*

It was too small to keep.
Two bites at best.
Not even enough for a fish taco.

I was going to raise it.

To become a full-sized fish taco?

Danielle laughs. She has such a funny laugh,
like someone sped up a video, fast and high-pitched.

No! For a pet!

You can't keep a bluegill for a pet, dork.

She throws the blankets down, sits up,
curly black hair a big mess from two days of camping.

Yes, I could!
I would have named it Danny.

Yeah, you could have dressed it in little
fish clothes and taken it for walks
in a portable aquarium on wheels.

We both crack up,
falling back onto our sleeping bags,
burying our heads in our pillows.

Then Danielle sits up again.
Her smile falls.
Her eyes widen.
She looks afraid.

What? What's wrong?

Danielle slowly raises an unsteady finger,
points at the wall of the tent.

There's something out there.

I turn, press my hand to the fabric.
It's cold and hard when it should be
warm and soft.

Hand still held to the tent wall,
I look back at Danielle.

It's a monster, Nora.

ONE LAST LIE

Please tell me the truth, Eleanor.
Who is the Beast?

Don't
Ever ask again.
My answer stands.
Once and for all, he's
Not real.

HE'S HERE

A clap of thunder,
and I'm back in the cave,
one sore hand pressed
to the cold stone wall.

I pull my hand away and see
a dark handprint when the sky
flickers with light.

The booms fill the cave,
and the flashes reveal
the cave is covered
with blood.

And now someone is climbing
up
the
canyon
wall.

I hear grunts,
rocks breaking loose
and falling to the canyon floor.

Closer.
Closer.
Closer.

He's here.

THINGS I DON'T TELL

The Beast
is dead, pale eyes
and jagged teeth
and sharp claws
and camouflaged exoskeleton
that glows
by the light of the moon
like the scorpions
under Dad's black light
that creep up our walls
and over our ceilings
and then drop
into our beds
and in the worst
of my nightmares
the Beast begins
to molt
his exoskeleton
to reveal
what is underneath

but I always
wake up
before I have
to know.

But I can't wake up
right now.

Because   I'm   not   asleep.

TWO CLAWS

Ground yourself, Eleanor.

But   all   I   feel   is   pain,   and
          all   I   smell   is   blood,
and all   I   taste   is   my   swollen
          tongue, and   bleeding lips,
                    and   all   I   hear   is   my
          pounding   heart   and   the   booms
moving   closer   and   his   ascent
                                        up
                                        the
                                        canyon
                                        wall.

A   flash   of   light,
and   a   snake is   here   going to   attack me.
I   kick   and   kick   and   kick
and   won't   let it   hurt me,
bring   one   foot   down   and   smash   it,
kick   it
       over

           the

               edge.

It's gone.   I killed it.   But then another burst   of lightning,
   and I see

      two   claws

   curving   the   edge
         over

   of   the   cave   to   grip   the   ground
where   remnants   of   my   blood   and   hair   remain.
   He's
   pulling
   himself
   up,
up   to   meet   me,   here   in   this   cave.

I   want   my   mom.
I   want   my   dad.
I   want   Danielle.

Rewrite your nightmare, Eleanor.

I   can't.
I'm   too   scared.
I   don't   have   the   strength.

Yes, you do.

GASPING AND GRASPING

I am
      panicking.

Breathing,
      breathing,
breathing,
      but can't
catch my breath.

Gasping,
      gasping,
gasping,
      but there's no air.

Lying
      on my side,
facing what is
      coming
         over
           the
              edge,
revealed only
      by
quick bursts
      of light.

Grasping,
      grasping,
grasping
      the stone floor,
as though
      my breath,
      the air,
is there,
      and I can
somehow find it.

Clenching
    my eyes shut
as the crackled exoskeleton
    of his face is
about to appear
      over
        the
          side.

Can't bear
    to see
my waking nightmare.

STRONG ENOUGH

And then I feel
a hand
instead of a claw
against my cheek.

Fingers soft and cool
against my burning skin.

I know this hand.

She is powerful
and fearless and brave.

Only my mother is strong enough
to scare the Beast away.

LET IT BE

Shhhhhhh,
she comforts me.
Shhhhhhh.

And she sings the song she always
sang when I was sick or scared
or simply not tired enough to fall asleep.

But I can't stand to hear
"Golden Slumbers" right now.

I can't stand it.

Please sing another song.

Her gentle fingertips
caress my forehead.
Okay,
she whispers.
Okay.

And somehow, despite being
out of my mind with sickness.

Despite the whole world
falling apart.

Despite the Beast waiting for me
down in the canyon.

Despite it all possibly, likely
coming to an end,
I am able to fall into a fevered sleep
inside a hole in a wall
on the side of a canyon
while my mother sings me
"Let It Be."

BEATLES DREAM

My mother is standing guard.
My mother keeps the Beast away.

And so I dream of her.
And I dream of Dad.
And I dream of the Beatles
because Mom loved their music.

I dream of my mother's funeral.
Dad had them play "In My Life"
because it was her song for him.
He had them play "Blackbird"
because it was her song for me.

I dream about my dad,
in his room, crying and sobbing
and weeping and wailing
while listening to "Yesterday."

I hate that song.

In the dream, I finally
walk into that room
and change the song
to "Hey Jude."

Then we sit together
in a beautiful, peaceful place
that could only exist in a dream
and listen to "Here Comes the Sun."

STILL HERE

The pain in my head,
pounding with venom and thirst,
awakens me.

Reaching a hand up to my matted hair,
I feel the tender lump on the back of my skull
where it hit the cave ceiling.

A tunnel of sparkling sunlight
shines down into the canyon.

How long was I sleeping?

It must be about noon.
Noon the next day.
The next day?
Please let it be only the next day.
Could I have slept longer?

I look at the cuts on my hands,
study the slices and scratches.
They still look fresh,
not yet scabbing.

A person can only go
about three days without water,
and I feel like I have
another day left in me.
I *must* have another day left.

So it *had* to be only one night.
That means it's been two nights,
forty-eight hours, since the flood.

I made it through another night.
So sick and dehydrated and starving,
but I'm still here.
I beat the Beast back
and I vanquished the venom
and I thwarted the thirst,
and I'm still here.

Pushing myself up to sit,
my stomach churns.
My limbs feel
like they're filled with sand.

I look around the cave.
Where is it?
I lean over, peer down,
and there it is
lying on the canyon floor.

The rope.

ALL FOR NOTHING

No, no, no.
The rope for which I sacrificed
my arms and legs and face and time
lies on the canyon floor
twenty feet below.

I kicked it, killed it,
shoved it over the edge,
so triumphant in my accomplishment,
in how I protected myself.

How will I ever get out of here
without my rope?

I can see the ground is dry.
No flood came.
I lie back down,
pull my knees up to my chest,
and cry tearless sobs.

THE ONLY PERSON IN THE WORLD

Forty-eight hours.
And Dad still hasn't found me.

What if he passed by while I slept?
What if he didn't see me?

No, he'd have seen my marks in the dirt,
the blood streaking the wall,
the hair scattered around.
He would have looked up.

He didn't come.

It's quiet except for my sobs.
I feel like the only person
left in the world.
I know I'm not, but I also know

Dad's   not coming   to   find me.

It will have to be me
who finds him.

UP

I push myself back up.
Muscles cramping, I grab
my brown, wadded tank top,
slip it over my head, and pull it down.

I drape my boots over my shoulder,
boot laces still tied together.

I lean out of the cave and look down again.
Then I turn my head to look up
toward the blinding blue sky.

It's not very far,
but my muscles are feeble,
weak from   dehydration,
               venom,
               lack of food.

I pull a mesquite bean out of my pocket
and bite down, chewing, but with so little
spit left, it's dust in my mouth.
I try to swallow, but it sticks in my dry throat,
making me cough, part of it coming back out,
part of it making its way down to my
hollow stomach.

This mouthful of sawdust is all
I have to energize me.

But there's nowhere to go from here
but up, even if it means
I may never get back down.

TIME TO GO

I sit here, chewing and coughing
on the dry beans,
wishing I could stay,
terrified of what I have to do to leave.
I reach a hand out of the cave,
and my fingertips just barely
skim the light.

I can't stay here,
where no one will find me.
I can't stay here,
when I'm the only one who can find Dad.

An insect flutters around outside the cave.
Focusing on it, I try
to slow the spinning in my head.

The insect soars into the cave
and settles on the floor beside me.
I'm surprised to see
it's a monarch butterfly.
I move my hand toward it,
and it flies away.

Time for me to do the same.

LEAVING

Sticking my head out once more,
I wait for my eyes to adjust to the light.
I look up the wall,
tell myself again it's not very far.
I've survived the flood,
the wind, the venom,
the hunger, the thirst.
I can do this.

Staying in this cave
is not an option.

~~I fell yesterday.~~
I won't fall today.

I did twenty feet yesterday.
I can do another twenty today.

Finding a foothold outside the cave,
I move sideways away from the opening
to follow another crack to the top

One more foothold,
my fingers gripping the crack,
and I'm nearly above the cave.

Now there's no going back in.

CLIMBING

I take my time.
My hair is no longer an obstacle,
and I have more light.

I feel,
read,
the rock wall with my toes
as though the route
is written in braille.

But I'm so very, very tired
and didn't realize how weak
muscles can be
because I've never gone
this long without eating
in my entire life.

The weakness
is in every part of me:
in my legs,

in my arms,
in my heart,
in my fingers
trying to hold on
to the narrow split
in the rock.
They tremble
and threaten release.

Now I feel the Beast below me,
sneering, sniping, snapping
his snarling mouth,
his claws outstretched,
waiting, patiently waiting,
for me to fall.

Climbing takes energy, strength, and patience.
What little I have left is as thin and frail
as the monarch's wings.

The most powerful thing I have
to fuel my climb is
anger.

GRIP STRENGTH

Grip strength is crucial, Dad says,
holding Mom's rope as she climbs,
keeping it taut.
She's almost at the top of the wall.

I'm six years old,
and we're standing in his rock gym
together.

You never know what you might face
in the desert, Dad says.
You have to be prepared for everything.

Mom reaches the top.
She waves down at us, bright and beaming.
Then she releases the wall
and leaps,
no fear, no worry, no doubt
that Dad will belay the rope for her properly.

No doubt
that Dad will always keep her safe.

Dad watches her descend,
slowly feeding the rope
through the belay device.
She lands
and throws her arms around him,
giving him a kiss
that makes me crinkle my nose.

Then she turns to me, runs a chalky hand
down my hair, tells me,
It's your turn now, my little blackbird.
Get ready to fly.

STRESS

I'm climbing using cracks
my fingers barely slip into
up to the first joint.

I'm climbing using protrusions
in the rock that may only stick out enough
to hold the tips of my toes.

My feet are sore, toes raw, toenails torn.
My hands are swollen, palms sliced,
fingers cracked, fingernails shredded to nubs.

At home, I eat my chocolate
and listen to my music
and wrap myself tightly in my soft blanket
and tie my figure eights
and knead my balloon of flour.

Mary told me how to make it:
a regular birthday balloon,
baking flour, and a funnel to fill it.

And I knead
and knead
and knead
until the balloon bursts.

Then I make another one.

There's no way I could hold on
to this wall of rock right now
with my marred hands
if I hadn't kneaded my balloon of flour
thousands and thousands of times.

THE TOP

My fingers finally brush the ground
above my head, and the relief almost
makes my tired limbs go limp,
which I can't allow.

My heart speeds with excitement
as I grip the edge of the canyon
and pull myself up, allowing my upper body
to rest on the hot dirt for a few seconds.

Forty feet.
Without rope,
without rock shoes,
without chalk,
without a harness,
without a belayer
standing at the bottom
taking up my slack
and keeping me safe so

I don't plummet to the earth.
Forty feet.

And   I   did   it.

DESERT SUN

I drag my legs up out of the canyon.
I pull my boots, socks still stuffed inside,
off my shoulder and slip them back on my
sore feet, wincing at the pain.

Our closest star bakes my skin,
dries my insides, and drains
the last drops of energy,
making muscles cramp.

The mud I'd slathered on my skin
for protection has mostly flaked off.
The back of my neck is already burning
without my long hair to protect it.
There's not even a single drop
of muddy water up here.
No canyon walls to block the sun.

But I don't have time to lament my
lost mud,
lost hair,
lost water,
lost shadows,
because I have to focus on finding my
lost dad.

REASON

I strain to see through squinted eyes,
black spots bursting all around me.

Nothing.
There's nothing,
not even power lines.
Nothing
but scrubby brittlebush
and scrawny palo verdes
and gangly ironwoods
and towering saguaros
as far as I can see.

Blisters sting my feet and toes,
and my feet ache
from so
      much
         walking.

I stumble and scrape my knees.
My hands scream out in pain
as rough dirt and stones
dig into my cuts and sores.

And again I pray for help,
for a plane to see,
for a hiker to come along,
for a nearby bush
to erupt into flame.

And then maybe they'd see.
And then maybe they'd come.
And then maybe I'd know
there is a reason for all of this.

FORGIVE

People say the desert is unforgiving,
as if it's a harsh judge who will
send you to prison for a tiny mistake.

People say respect the desert,
as if it's a big muscular bully who will
pummel you for the slightest misstep.

They're right.

And I've made so many missteps.
I'm supposed to find a shady spot
during the day to rest and only travel by night.

I stop in front of a large palo verde,
consider curling up under its skinny branches,
barely large enough to filter the beating sun,
then moving on after dark.

If only there were moonlight or a flashlight for that.
If only there were time for that.

I don't know what's happening with Dad,
where he is, what condition he's in,
but I'm certain now that
every
second
counts.

If it were summer,
we'd be dead already.

But we would never hike a canyon
in the middle of the Sonoran Desert
in the middle of summer.

And so I hope the desert forgives
my missteps, mistakes, my mild disrespect.

Despite the heat mirages
wavering all around me,
despite the turkey vultures
now circling above me as I walk,
floating on their invisible whirlpools,
I hope the desert
doesn't judge me too harshly.

I hope the desert forgives.

ANOTHER WAY

I walk along the precipice,
watching the ground for rattlesnakes.
They'll be out,
and stepping on one would mean
the end of all of this.

I periodically scan the canyon for Dad
with no good idea how I'll get back down to him
without the rope.

I stop in front of a large ocotillo,
its branches long wands,
wondering whether I could somehow use one.
But even the tallest wand is probably
only a third as tall as the canyon.
Dad could climb a little, grab on to it.
The thorns would pierce his hands
the whole way.
They would pierce mine as I held it.
The pain would be unreal.
Could it, could I, hold his weight?

Could I use a tree branch?
The palo verde,
the mesquite,
the ironwood,
all   have   large   thorns,
and their branches aren't nearly long enough.

The rib of a saguaro skeleton?
I haven't seen one,
and they're probably too brittle.

Could I use another kind of plant?
Weave a rope like the Tohono O'odham
weave their beautiful baskets?
What do they use?
I've learned about this so many times
at national parks, museums, art shows, and classes.
Yucca? Devil's claw? Bear grass?
I can't remember, but I know
I've seen none of that.
And how long would that take anyway?
To weave a forty-foot rope?
Too long.

What if Dad isn't even in the canyon?
What if he's already climbed out?
What if we've somehow
missed each other?
And I'm walking in the hot sun,
no water to be found.

Walking to nowhere and no one.

WALKING ON WATER

I keep replaying it in my mind.
I can see and feel the backpack
slipping from my fingers
over and over again.
The weight of it.
The weight of the water within.

I should never have climbed to that cave.
Even if a flood had come, drowning
would have been better than this dehydration.

My need is so intense, I would do anything
to be floating in the black water right now,
water filling and spilling into my mouth and throat
and even my lungs.

There's water under my feet.
Beneath the hard, hot desert ground,
the underneath is filled with endless aquifers.
Despite literally walking on water
to find my dad, I can't drink a single drop
from underneath.

DESPERATION

I now carry the dry desert
on my skin,
in my eyes,
in my nose,
in my mouth.

Dust coats the inside of my cheeks
and the surface of my teeth.
A cactus clogs my throat.
Sand covers my tongue.
It's a wonder I don't disintegrate
into a puff of powder.

I see a pop of pink ahead,
and my wobbly legs automatically speed up.

Please, please, please...

I almost collapse in relief at the sight
of prickly pear, the last
few fall fruits clinging to the plant,
the rest having been eaten and carried away
by birds and beetles and javelinas.

Dad and I used to pick the fruit together
to make prickly pear Popsicles,
sweet and cold and refreshing,
the taste like watermelon.

Dad's instructions were strict
to save me from the spines.

> *Always, always use tongs*
> *to pull the fruit off the plant.*

I grasp the fruit in my bare hands,
tearing it from the green paddles,
the small, nearly invisible, hairlike spines
getting into every inch of my skin.

> *Watch out for the bigger needles.*

A large spine pierces my tender hand,
going deep enough to draw blood
when I tear it out.

> *You have to open the fruit carefully,*
> *with gloves, a sharp knife,*
> *a spoon to lift the fruit out.*

I drop the fruit on the ground
and smash it with my boot,
then I pry it open
with my thorn-filled fingers
and suck the meager warm fruit out.

> *Never put it in your mouth*
> *until all the small spines are gone,*
> *or you'll be very, very sorry.*

The needles find their way
into my lips and mouth and gums
and tongue and cheeks,
juice staining all it touches
in flaming fuchsia.

Everything in the desert has thorns.
Everything in the desert hurts you.

> *Strain the fruit to remove*
> *the stone-hard seeds.*

I   eat   every   last   fruit
skin and spines
and seeds and all,
not willing to waste
a single drop
by spitting any of it
on the ground.

I can't get enough.
I could never get enough.
I swallow mouthful after mouthful,
my stomach filling with stones.
I'd have to eat about a thousand fruits
to satisfy my need.

The flavor brings me back
to those icy cold Popsicles.
The three of us sitting on the porch
dripping hot pink everywhere
while Mom reads us her newest poem.

I want to cry, but don't.
I have to move on,
my thirst barely muffled
by what I've just done to myself.

UNDERNEATH

A dust devil spins
across the landscape
like a small tornado.
I watch it as I walk,
wishing it were made
of water like a waterspout.
I would dive inside it and let it
twist me, twirl me, whisk me away.

The devil moves in my direction,
or my own feet are carrying me
toward the column of dust,
as though I'm not controlling them,
as though they have a mind of their own
and that mind believes
there's water in the whirlwind.

Water.

Not just to drink, but to dive.
I remember swimming with my mom
in our pool in the desert.
The coconutty smell of sunblock.
The sounds of splashing
and her voice, like the sun's warm embrace
on my skin.

My hair soaks up every ray
and heats to burning.
My toes sting
on the terribly named cool decking,
and I dip them in the refreshing blue.

And then I jump into the cold water,
the relief against my hot scalp so intense
it gives me chills.
The feel of chlorine in my eyes.
The blurred sounds and images of the underneath
when I tried to stay under as long as possible,
challenging myself to hold my breath always longer,
my mom worried I wasn't coming back up.

I reach the dust devil,
and it envelopes my body for only a second
before dissolving back to the desert.

I take in a lungful of dust and stop, double over,
heaving and coughing.
I can barely breathe until every grain is gone.

I stand back up, wipe at my sand-filled eyes,
and continue along the edge.

I feel as though I'm in the underneath now,
images all blurry, holding my breath.
But without the coolness of the water to soothe
my burning cheeks, blazing scalp, battered body.

And without my mom here to worry
that I won't be coming back up.

DANIELLE

The mirages are all around me.
I'm so thirsty I can almost believe,
convince myself, tell myself,
they're really water, even though
I also know that's impossible,
that the desert is now tricking me,
taunting me, teasing me
with its terrible heat waves.

Water.

If only I were floating in the hot night
with Danielle, our feet splashing
outside our tubes, talking endlessly
about boys and books and movies and makeup
and what we want to do when we're older.
Maybe I'll be a park ranger.
Maybe Danielle will be a stylist.

If I were there, I would drink the whole pool.

If only that could happen again,
that we could be there again,
floating and talking and laughing and splashing.
If only that hadn't stopped.
How could I have let that stop?
How could I—

A wave of dizziness overcomes me,
sends me stumbling toward
the edge, and for a split second,
I think I'll tumble right over it,
not sure where solidness ends
and emptiness begins.

I fall to the ground on my butt,
only inches from the drop-off.
I sit in the hot dirt and wait
for the dizziness to pass,
my sunburned face in my mangled hands.

If Danielle would ever be my friend again,
I'd have nothing left to give her now.
Nothing but skin,
burned, torn, and pierced with thorns.
Nothing but hair,
chopped, tattered, and matted with mud.
Nothing but this thirst,
overwhelming, overpowering, overtaking me.

I know, I know, I know
she wouldn't ask for more than that.

She never, ever asked for anything
but me.

TRUTH

Danielle sits on my bed in my room,
squeezing one of my pillows to her chest,
tears running down her glistening brown cheeks.

I don't know how to help you, Nora.

    You can't.

I want to help you.

    You can't.

I'm trying to understand.

    You can't!
    You can't!
    You can't!

I scream at her over and over again,
my eyes clenched shut,
hands clamped over my ears.

I hate her right now.
She loves me,
and I hate her
because she can't understand.
Because it happened
to me and not her.

And so I scream.

        You can't!
        You can't!
        You can't!
        Go away!
        Go away!
        Go away!

I scream it long enough
that when I finally stop and open my eyes,

she's gone.

And when she calls later that day,
I don't answer.

When she calls the next day,
I don't answer.

When she calls the day after that,
I don't answer.

Danielle chose to leave my life
because it was the only choice
I   gave   her.

LIMINAL SPACE

Time between what was
and whatever might come next
is liminal space.

IN-BETWEEN

After it happened, I thought everyone would be
impacted, altered, changed forever.

But everyone else was exactly the same.

Dad and I were the only ones who were
impacted, altered, changed forever.
I didn't know
what to do,
how to act,
who to be,
in the in-between space
of what was and what might be.

I only knew for sure what would
never be again.

COME BACK

I force myself up.
I continue walking.
I move forward.

Eleanor, sometimes people who have experienced
a traumatic event come back
even more resilient than they were before.

There's no excuse for giving up.
I have to keep trying.
Even when I once more veer
toward the edge.
Even when my knees
begin to buckle.
Even when the black spots
dance in my eyes,
I have to never stop trying.

I can come back from this.
I want to live.
And I want Dad to live.

The clouds are moving in,
the desert sky growing ever darker,
giving me some relief
from the burning sun.
I'm grateful for every cloud.

The refreshing smell of creosote
suddenly fills the air and my lungs.
It gives me the tiniest boost,
clears my clogged mind,
drains an ounce of lead from my legs.

It's raining again.
Not here. Not over me.
Somewhere.

But even if it didn't rain
for a very long time,
the creosote bush would survive.
It can live up to two years
without water.

The creosote drops its leaves.
It may even drop its branches,
but it keeps what it needs in the root crown,
so it can come back.

I've shed leaves.
I've even torn away branches,
but I still have what I need in my root crown.
And so I can come back.

I've survived this last year.
I've gone half as long as the creosote bush.
I can go another year.
But I want this year to be different.
I don't want to survive the next year
as I did the last year.
I want to live the next year.

I can come back.

237

WONDERSTRUCK

The afternoon sun pauses all movement,
making the desert still and vast and quiet
around me while I walk.

I have to tell myself to keep putting
one foot in front of the other.
Even when the only thought in my mind
is to lie down somewhere, curl up under a tree,
and sleep forever, I have to keep putting
one foot in front of the other.

And then I'm stopped,
my legs and my heart.

An animal stands
at the edge of the canyon,
looking down into it.
It turns its face to me.

My heart resumes pounding
as I try to make out what it is
through sanded, sun-scorched eyes.
Mountain lion?
Coyote?
Bobcat?
It can probably sense
that I'm weak, nearing my end,
unable to fight back.

But it only stands there,
as still as I am.

I focus my eyes as well as I can.
Too small for a mountain lion.
Looks like a coyote
but
reddish legs and underside,
white throat,
long, bushy tail with a black tip,
sun glowing pink through its
pointy, triangular ears.

A fox.

I stay as still as possible,
no longer scared, but because
I don't want to scare *it* away
It tilts its head at me,
watches me with curiosity,
with wariness.
It doesn't seem to understand
what I am.

The desert surrounding us
is as still and vast and quiet
as my mind, and I am
wonderstruck
to see a fox in the desert.

I wish Dad were here.

I stretch out my hand,
and that's all it takes
to scare the fox away.

But as though I somehow
summoned Dad
with the power of my wishing,
I look down into the canyon,
and
there he is.

SO CLOSE

I've found him.

I open my mouth to call out to him.
Nothing but a rasp escapes because
I screamed my voice away last night.

He lies on his stomach,
his head turned toward me.

His eyes
    sealed shut with mud.
His clothing
    torn to shreds.
His skin
    burned and sanded off.
His hair
    patchy and matted with mud and blood.
His left arm
    contorted strangely behind him.
His backpack
    still on and in one piece.

I've found him.
Finally.
I've reached him.

He's so close, so close
I could stretch out a hand
and nearly touch him,
washed up on a ledge
about five feet below me.

No, not washed up.
I see the trail of handprints and boot prints
and streaks of mud and blood
where he dragged himself
up a series of outcroppings until he reached
this ledge just large enough to hold him.

But with his injured leg
and his now twisted arm,
I imagine he couldn't make
the final five feet of flat wall.

Or maybe he just collapsed onto his stomach,
unable to breathe, his lungs filled with mud.
Unable to see, his eyes filled with mud.

So very close.
I just need to drop down to reach him,
to reach his backpack.

There's barely enough room for me,
enough that I could drop down
and not fall off the side if I'm careful.

All I have to do is swing my legs down
and drop the last few feet onto the ledge with him.

He's so close.

But I'm on the
wrong side
of the canyon.

TWITCH

I fall
to the ground.

I cover
my aching eyes.

I don't want to see,
but I have to look,
need to know.

I watch Dad
through splayed fingers.
    So still.
I watch Dad.
     Still like death.

I open my mouth.
    Dad.
But no sound escapes.

In a hole in a canyon wall,
I screamed my voice away.
It drifted over the side
and into the canyon,
where it might remain forever.

I look up to the sky and I see turkey vultures
circling above Dad in the same way
they've been following me.

They are above him, but
they haven't yet *landed* on him,
haven't started pecking at him.

I drop my hands from my face,
jump back to my feet,
strain to focus my eyes on Dad.
My heart pounds expectantly
as I concentrate all my energy
on watching him
for any small movement.

And then I see it.

Twitch.
Twitch.
Twitch.

Is it real? Am I imagining it?
I don't think so because
I *feel* it.

That finger twitch vibrates the air
in the canyon between us.
It sends waves of energy
through the atmosphere
until they reach my body and infuse it,
like a river flooding a dry wash,
with the will to go on.

The will to do what I know
I need to do.

DEAD

I stand at the edge
   of the precipice,
      threshold,
         abyss.

There's no way for me to get down
the vertical wall on this side.
No one climbs down.

If I hadn't pushed my rope
back into the canyon,
I could have tied it to something
to lower myself,
then climbed back up to Dad
on the other side.

I spot a tree lying on the canyon floor,
not far from Dad.
An uprooted, *dead* tree,
drying for the last two days
in the hot desert air
and cold canyon winds.

My eyes move from one side
of the canyon to the other
as Dad's words echo in my mind.

> *I think you could jump it.*

ACCEPTANCE

Acceptance of self,
in order to fully heal,
is necessary.

GUILT

It's easy to feel guilty, Eleanor,
when you have nothing at all to feel guilty about.

Mom and Dad only thought of me.
Sofía Moreno must have thought of her boys,
though I can never ask her.

I only thought of myself.

You did nothing wrong.
The other people hiding did nothing wrong.
Only one person did something wrong.

MORE

I've searched in this desert

               above myself,
        beside myself,
            below myself

to find myself.

What have I found?

I'm more
than what one person did to me.

I'm more
than this past year.

I still have more
to do with my life.

More that is good.
More that is important.
More that is worth doing.

How can there ever be more
if I don't fight for it
until the very end?

COMPLICATED

I'm scared of doing this.
Maybe I'm even crazy for doing this.

Crazy like
shoving your daughter under a table
instead of running away.

Crazy like
pushing your daughter up a canyon wall
instead of running away.

Crazy like
running at a shooter
instead of running away.

Crazy like
jumping over a canyon
instead of running away.

NIGHTMARE REWRITTEN

Booms
> all around me from the thunder
> closing in on us from the mountains.

Blood
> covering my hands, my arms, my legs,
> my head, my father, the canyon.

> And, of course, *he* is here for this.

> My wall is quaking.
> The bricks shudder
> and the stones break loose
> as I let it all
> crumble to the ground.

> And now there is nothing
> between me and the

Beast.

I turn away from the edge of the canyon.
He follows closely behind.

I leave the edge of the canyon;
I'll need the distance.

A BLUR OF BROWN LEGS

She's not here for this rewrite.

Sofía Moreno,
just a regular mom,
with two little boys
in the booth next to ours.

Sofía Moreno,
who tackled a shooter
intent on killing
as many as possible.

Sofía Moreno,
who died
while giving her two boys,
    while giving everyone,
    while giving me,
a chance,
    a bigger chance,
a moment,
    a longer moment,
to flee,
to hide,
to act,
to survive.

HE FOLLOWS

How far do I need?

> *You're strong, Eleanor.*

Far enough to gather speed.

> *You're resilient.*

Not so far that I wear myself out.

> *That's not something you're born with.*

I stop about a hundred feet from the canyon.

> *It's something you learn.*

I crouch down
and tighten my boot laces.

> *You have to believe.*

I look up at the graying sky.

Believe you can succeed.

I turn and face the canyon.

Believe in yourself.

I close my eyes and take a deep breath,
slow, steady, controlled.

Even when it feels hopeless.

I open my eyes to see
the shadow of the Beast
creep up beside me.

Even when you're afraid.

I watch as the dark outline
of his exoskeleton
molts and drops
to the ground
with a nauseating,
crackling,
wet
crunch.

> *Even when you are*
> *absolutely terrified.*

And I know now
what is underneath.

But it's not who I expected.

> *Don't be defined by your post-traumatic stress.*

I move my eyes
away from the Beast's shadow
to the canyon in front of me.

> *Be defined by your post-traumatic growth.*

REWRITING

It's amazing
what can happen to a first draft
when you rewrite it,
how characters can change,
how much they can grow,
the incredible things they can accomplish.

You can't judge a
story,
     dream,
poem,
     nightmare
by the first draft.

And if you're able
to find the strength,
you can completely rewrite it.

FREEDOM

I sprint as fast as my
weak,
envenomated,
dehydrated,
exhausted
body can carry me.

I run from hopelessness   toward hope.
    I run from shame   toward acceptance.
      I run from hate   toward love.
      I run from anger   toward peace.
    I run from the Beast   toward freedom.

But he's chasing me now.

    Not fast enough.

I see his malformed shadow
moving closer.

Not strong enough.

He is right behind me.

Not brave enough.

I feel Desolation's putrid breath on
my sunburned neck.

Not powerful enough.

Decay's rotting, pale, bony fingers
dig into my arm.

Not enough.

Despair will take me
before I can make it.

*No. That is a lie,
and he is the liar.*

*I am *fast* enough.*

I pick up speed
as I near
the canyon's edge.

I am faster than the Beast.

He releases his grip
on my arm.

I am stronger than the Beast.

He pants from weakness.

I am braver than the Beast.

He whimpers from fear.

I am more powerful than the Beast.

The
blur of brown legs,
    the legs of the person who saves me
    in my rewritten nightmare, are
mine,
    covered in dried blood and mud.

No matter where I land...

Wait too long,
and I will fly into the canyon
instead of over it.

No matter where I land...

Jump too soon,
and I will never make the distance.

No matter where I land,

I am leaving the Beast
on this side of the canyon
forever.

GROWTH

Self-efficacy.
Belief that I can succeed.
Post-traumatic growth.

FLYING

I fly.

Across the divide
that separates Dad and me.

Across space and time.

Across the universe.

Over the ruins
of my crumbled wall.

Out of the past
and into the future.

BLACKBIRD

My mother called me Blackbird.
She said,

> *Because you're waiting*
> *for that moment when you*
> *finally believe in yourself.*
> *That's when you'll arise.*
> *That's when you'll fly.*

Even now she's here,
lifting me up.

Her love,
her belief,
her courage,
her beauty,
gives me flight,
carries me on the desert wind
to the other side of healing.

LANDING

I land
on the other side of the canyon.

I roll
over and over.

My right knee strikes
a rock and explodes in pain.

I am
finally still.

I am
on the other side of the canyon.

I am
alive.

My knee
   shattered.
My skin
   tattered.
My head
   throbbing.
Rocks and thorns
   embedded in my flesh.
My chest
   constricted.
But

I

am

ALIVE.

DEFEATED

Lying on my side in the hot rocky dirt,
my head resting on one outstretched arm,
I gaze across the canyon at the Beast.

He is nothing but a white mirage,
pacing angrily along the ledge,
looking for a way across the divide.

But I've created a boundary
he can't cross.

My boundary is not a leaky wall made
   of   shame
and   anger
and   guilt
and   fear
and   hate.

My boundary

is

a

C
A
N
Y
O
N.

STRENGTH

I sit up, begin to bend my legs to stand,
and a knife stabs deep into my knee.
I let out a silent scream
as the pain shoots from my right knee
into the rest of my leg.

Trying to put pressure
on only my left leg to stand,
my whole body wobbles,
falls back to the ground,
more stabbing pain in my knee.

And so I push myself on my butt
backward with my left leg,
the hot, rocky dirt torture
against my sore, thorn-filled hands,
dragging my right leg,
every movement a piercing pain.

I pull myself to the edge.

I no longer have
the anger to fuel me,
so I draw strength
from love
as I prepare for
all
      the
           pain.

Lying on my stomach,
I draw strength from Danielle.

    Danielle,
    who taught me how
    to bake snickerdoodles,
    to braid a fishtail,
    to dive.

    Danielle,
    who loved me even
    when I was full of hate.

    Danielle,
    who I hope still loves me
    and will let me back in.

Lowering my legs over the edge,
I draw strength from Mom.

> Mom,
> who loved writing
> and inspired me to write.

> Mom,
> who will always be with me
> in my head,
> in my heart,
> in my poems.

> Mom,
> who pushed me to safety
> at Café Ardiente.

> Mom,
> who, even as the bullets
> tore her apart,
> told me she loved me.

Gripping the edge of the canyon,
I draw strength from Dad.

Dad,
who taught me to climb
walls of stone.

More skin tears away
from my ruined hands.

Dad,
who taught me to pull
food and water from mud,
from mesquite beans,
from prickly pear fruit.

I look down, attempt to
pinpoint a landing place.
I don't want to land on him,
but there's so little room
on that ledge for both of us.

Dad,
who pushed me to safety
in the canyon.

This will be my last time
going into the canyon.
And I know I won't
make it back out without help.

Dad,
who, even as the floodwaters
tore him apart,
told me he loved me.

TOGETHER

My leg hits Dad's legs first.
My ankle twists
as I lose my footing.
I stumble,
fall on top of him,
then roll
onto the small sliver
of rocky ledge,
barely large enough
to hold me,
grasping his backpack,
frantic
not to slip off the side,
the pain in my knee
so intense,
I lay my head on Dad
and black out.

PULSE

I come to,
leg throbbing with more pain
than I knew possible.
I don't want to look at it.
I don't want to see
what's become of my knee.

I grasp Dad's
tattered, shredded clothes
to pull myself up to his face.
I hold a finger under his dirt-clogged nose,
but I can't feel anything on my ragged skin.

Dropping my head,
I press my forehead against his.

    I found you.

And I listen.

    I'm here.

And I search,
barely able to keep my eyes open.

And then
I
see
a
pulsing
in his temple.

A slow
pulse.
A barely there
pulse.
A nearly finished
pulse.

Am I imagining it?

No.

I push myself up and look
at my father.

Alive.

HOPE

I open Dad's backpack
and scramble through the supplies.
Finding the canteen, I open it
with shaking fingers
and greedily guzzle, gulp,
choke myself on the warm water.
I have to force myself
to leave some for Dad.
I pour careful drops
on his mouth, but they glide right over,
pool on the ledge under his face,
and he doesn't wake up.

I push the canteen aside
and continue searching through the backpack.
I find the lighter, but I can't use it.
There's nothing to light here on this ledge
except a few small twigs.
And the uprooted, dead tree
is too far away.

I pull out what I really need.

I don't want to use it,
but it's all I have left.

I don't want to use it,
but I've reached my end.

I don't want to use it,
but this thing
does not control me.

I know the risks
if I do this.
I know the risks
if I don't do this.

I lie back and stare at the sky,
now shrouded in gray clouds.

I debate
what I've already
decided.
But it's a losing argument.

There is only
one thing
that will draw them quickly.
One thing
everyone fears in the desert.

The planes are above the cloud cover.
They won't see.
And even if there weren't gray clouds,
I doubt they would see anyway.

What would it give us?
A small chance.
A short moment.
I have to give us a bigger chance.
A longer moment.

It could rain soon.
I am out of time
in every way.

They'll be watching.
They'll be on high alert
because of all the lightning.

I hope it won't spread,
that the wind won't carry an ember
up out of the canyon.

I hope they
see.
I hope they
come.
I hope they
understand.
I hope they
forgive.

But the most important thing is that
I hope.

And because
I hope,
I roll onto my stomach
on the sliver of ledge,
my knee screaming at me,
and stretch out my arms.

I hold the flare gun in both hands
and point it into the canyon.

I pull back on the hammer,
but it won't budge,
and I worry that I don't have
enough strength left
in even one finger
to do what I need to do.

I stare at the gun until I figure out
how to turn the safety off.

I pull back on the hammer again,
and it clicks into place.

I hold the gun once more
in both hands,
arms outstretched,
pointed at the dead, uprooted tree.

My finger trembles
as I squeeze
and press
and pull the trigger.

CLOSING

The gun blasts my ears,
blinds my eyes,
jumps in my hands.
I try to hold on to it,
but it slips from my fingers
and plunges into the canyon.

It's gone.

I twist onto my side and once more
press my forehead to Dad's,
my arm draped over him,
my ears buzzing,
dark smears across my vision.

I try to stay awake.
I don't have the energy to look.
I barely have the energy to keep
my eyes open at all.

FIRE

And then
I smell smoke.

I hear crackling.

And I allow my eyes
to finally close
with the comforting knowledge
that I have set
that damn canyon
on fire.

MOM

Mom, Dad, me.

We sit around a smoking, crackling campfire
in folding chairs in the middle of the desert.

Mom wraps an arm around me to keep me warm
while Dad roasts us marshmallows.

He hands her one, and she pops it into my mouth,
so I don't have to take off my gloves.

Dad pulls another marshmallow off a stick and says,
I had a dream I was eating a giant marshmallow last night.

Mom looks down at me, raises an eyebrow.

Handing her the marshmallow, he says,
When I woke up my pillow was gone.

Mom and I look at each other,
our mouths full of marshmallow.
I snort as she rolls her eyes and gives me her
what-am-I-supposed-to-do-with-him look.

Why did the elephant sit on the marshmallow?
Dad asks.

Mom chews her marshmallow, swallows it.
Why?

And her voice is like a beam of warm sunlight
in a cold, dark cave.

To keep from falling in the hot chocolate.

Mom and I giggle,
and the sound of her laughter is like
fresh water trickling through the dry desert.

She squeezes me to her, leans down, whispers,
I love you. I'm proud of you.

It's real,
even if it is a dream.

It's real.

CRESCENDO

The canyon winds
are blowing again.

The canyon walls
are vibrating again.

A deafening sound
fills my ears.

I squeeze my arm around Dad,
my forehead still pressed to his.

It's okay.

Sand and pebbles break free
of the walls and tumble on top of us.

I'm here.

A crescendo builds
as the canyon threatens
to come apart around us.

> *Whatever's coming,*
> *we'll face it together.*

And then...

STILL FIGHTING

A crack in the darkness.

I look up
into the blinding light.

A whirring windmill
hovering in the sky.

The dark outline of a person
looking out from the helicopter.

I raise one
stained, thorn-filled, shredded hand
to show them

I'm still here.
I'm still alive.
I'm still fighting.

And then being lifted.

Up.
Up.
Up.

Out of the canyon,
toward the light,
a beautiful, terrifying, blinding light,
in the middle
of a cold, dark desert night.

PART

THREE

I put down my notebook and take a drink of water to soothe my throat, dry from reading aloud for so long.

Dad doesn't speak. He's been staring out the window, motionless except to wipe his cheeks every now and then, his left arm in a sling, draped over the couch's armrest.

Finally, he whispers, "Thank you."

I push myself off the couch and hop on one leg to my backpack. I slip the notebook back in and zip it up. "You're welcome," I say.

"I'll...," Dad says, trailing off.

"You'll what?"

"I'll have more to say later," he manages to get out.

Dad grabs the keys while I put my backpack on, then we make our way out to the Jeep. With my leg in a brace and Dad's arm in a sling, everything is a challenge for us. I clumsily flop toward my seat, and he nearly falls over, laughing, trying to keep me balanced with one arm. "We're a sorry pair, aren't we?" he says down to me.

I shake my head and smile up at him. "Nah. I don't think we're sorry at all."

He's still mostly quiet as we drive. It's not far. We've made this drive many, many times.

Dad stops the Jeep and walks around so he can help me. After I get out, I reach back to grab my backpack and crutches.

"Do you want me to walk you up?" Dad asks.

I stare at the house. "No. I can do this on my own."

Dad smiles, touches a lock of my hair, which I'd had evened out into a pixie cut. "I think you could do just about anything on your own." He puts his arm around me and whispers, "Good luck."

Dad walks back around the Jeep. He gets in, but he doesn't leave as I slowly make my way on crutches up the familiar walkway, swinging my injured leg. The weight of the notebook in my backpack is heavy on my shoulder.

I think about how I used to believe my life would only ever have two parts: Before and After. Now my life has three parts: Before, After, and After After. I look forward to the parts still to come.

I lean on one crutch when I get to the door, trying to keep my balance. I reach one healing hand out and ring the doorbell.

After a minute, she opens the door halfway, a tentative look on her face. There's surprise in her eyes, then sadness and wonder as she scans me over, taking in my short hair, the leg brace, the endless scrapes, scabs, and scratches slowly transforming into bright pink scars.

She sees all of it. She sees all of me. As she always has.

She opens the door widely for me now, and I hear Dad start the engine. The sounds of the Jeep fade as he drives away.

And Danielle lets me back in.

ACKNOWLEDGMENTS

On a blazing hot July day in 2017, my family and I ventured up to Payson to visit my mom and go hiking. We trekked through a canyon to a swimming hole called Water Wheel and had a nice time. Only a few days later, a large family from my hometown of Cave Creek visited that same canyon. A flash flood surprised the family, taking nine of them from this world. I've never been able to stop thinking about them, even though I didn't know them. The loss is unfathomable to me, and so I wrote this story partly as an expression of my grief for that family, but also for everyone who has suffered great losses in the blink of an eye.

Thank you to my editors, Lisa Yoskowitz and Hannah Milton, for challenging me to write every scene, page, and line better. Thank you to Karina Granda and

Pascal Campion for my beautiful cover. And to everyone else at Little, Brown Books for Young Readers who has supported me and my book—Michelle Campbell, Jackie Engel, Jen Graham, Stefanie Hoffman, Rosanne Lauer, Alvina Ling, Katie Boni, Lelia Mander, Sherri Schmidt, Christie Michel, Victoria Stapleton, and many more: Thank you from the bottom of my heart.

A good literary agent is invaluable, and I'm so grateful to my agent, Shannon Hassan, for always supporting me, listening to my *many* story ideas, reading everything I write (frequently multiple times), and helping to guide me.

Thank you to amazing middle-grade friends who read early drafts of the manuscript and provided valuable feedback: Jarrett Lerner, Sally J. Pla, and Heidi Lang. To the three best writing friends in the world: Stephanie Elliot, Kelly DeVos, and Lorri Phillips. And to Dr. Blasingame at ASU for supporting local writers and for supplying me with a constant stream of interns willing to do my bidding.

The only reason I have a job is because of the many booksellers, educators, and librarians who have supported me since my first book was released. Thank you for recommending my books to children. I can't tell you how much that means to me.

Thank you to family members who have supported me throughout my writing journey: Peggy Williams, Becky Self, Jennifer Kindle, and my mom, Gail Daggett. To my three daughters for inspiring me to write stories about strong girls.

I couldn't have accomplished what I have without the constant support of my husband, Zach Bowling, who takes care of our children and home while I chase this writing dream. Thank you, God, for all of it.

TURN THE PAGE FOR A SNEAK PREVIEW OF THE NEXT
THRILLING ADVENTURE STORY FROM DUSTI BOWLING

NOW

IT'S SO HOT TODAY IN DOWNTOWN PHOENIX, I COULD probably bake cookies in a car. Mom and I did that once—baked chocolate chip cookies in our car. The cookies weren't browned around the edges like when they're baked in an oven. They had mostly melted into a pale hard crust, but they were crumbly and totally cooked through. That was, of course, when we *had* a car.

Racing down the city sidewalk in the middle of summer, I feel crumbly and totally cooked through. Speeding cars and buses blast air in my face hot enough to bake *me*, or at least melt me into a pale crust. My stomach growls, and I wish I had a cookie with a giant glass of cold milk. I'd even settle for a car-baked cookie.

I stop at a bench shaded by a big sign for discount car insurance and breathe for a second, wiping the sweat from my forehead and shifting my backpack full of books from one aching shoulder to the other. If only I had a computer and internet at home, I wouldn't have to make this blazing-hot walk today.

When I finally reach the library, I burst through the automatic sliding doors and stop in the entry between those book-thief-detector things. I breathe in as much cool, book-scented air as my lungs can hold. The feel of the air-conditioning blowing against my sticky skin is almost worth the whole walk.

"Excuse me," someone behind me says. I hunch my shoulders and quickly move out of the way without looking. I rush to the drinking fountain and chug a ton of water before heading to the bathroom, where I throw my backpack on the counter and splash water over my face.

I soak up the sweat under my tight purple tank top and armpits with a wad of paper towels and pull my messy, damp, dark hair up into a bun without looking at myself in the mirror. I leave the bathroom, tugging my tank top down to cover my stomach, but it's too short. Everything I own is at least two sizes too small, which I'm constantly reminded of by the kids at school and by my eternal wedgie.

I slip the travel books I borrowed last week into the return slot, then go to the holds shelf, where several more are waiting for me. I'm not exactly the fastest reader, but when it comes to travel books, the pictures are really the most important thing. I love imagining I could jump inside them and explore all the far-off places.

The computers are mostly taken up by the homeless people using the library as a hiding place from the heat, but I manage to find an open one and set my stuff down. I log in using my library card number and go straight to BlipStream's website. I click on the only show in my favorites and wait for *The Desert Aviator* to begin. Addie usually starts the show around ten o'clock, but never on the dot. I wish Addie would record her episodes so I could watch them anytime, but if I want to see her show, I have to catch it while it's livestreaming.

Since the screen is dark, I hurry to the reference shelves and pull out this great atlas of Arizona, which has a map of the Alamo Lake area. Addie doesn't know that *I* know where she flies. She's never told me—I guess since we've never met in person. For all she knows, I could be some old guy who smells like cheese and onions pretending to be a twelve-year-old girl. So she never tells me where she flies or lives or goes to school or even what her real name is, but that's okay. We still tell each other lots of important stuff.

Figuring out where Addie flies has been fun. It makes me feel like Marie Tharp, who mapped the ocean floor, or Kira Shingareva, who mapped the *moon*. Alamo Lake isn't exactly the moon, but it's pretty cool to discover something, even if it's something small. Even if I'm not the first person to discover it.

But what I really wish is that I could be like Eva Dickson, the first woman to drive a car across the

Sahara. Eva was also an aviator, like Addie. If I had a plane or a car or even a motorcycle (and if I wasn't twelve and could drive and maybe had some money and food and a GPS and stuff like that), I'd travel to Alamo Lake and explore the whole area where Addie flies.

My life is so filled with *If I had*s that it sometimes feels like I'm drowning in them.

I remove the folded square of paper from my backpack and spread it on the desk. It's taken me a whole month to make this map, and I hope maybe even Kira Shingareva wouldn't think it completely stinks up the place.

My map shows the whole lake area with several mines, two canyons, three ghost towns, a hundred-year-old graveyard, native ruins, a bunch of trails, and all of Addie's takeoff and landing spots—stuff that can't be found on any other maps. When Addie starts her show, I'll be able to follow her, not just on the screen, but on my map.

Addie is definitely one of the youngest explorers I've discovered, and I wish I could be more like her— brave and daring enough to go on an adventure. But real adventures aren't like the movies. Real adventures are kind of scary. Lots of people die while exploring and mapping things. They get all kinds of diseases and broken bones and snakebites. They freeze to death and fall off mountains. And this one guy died from a *pimple*. It's true. Totally true.

I already have a few potentially killer pimples on my forehead, and I don't think I could face venomous snakes. Or even, like, a rabid raccoon. It would probably scare me to death. Then again, I don't think there are raccoons in the desert. A hungry pack rat would be pretty scary, though. It might have some kind of disease. And sharp teeth. Definitely sharp teeth.

I tap my knuckles on the desk, but the screen is still dark, even though it's now 10:04. Staring at the monitor, I open a new window. In the search box, I type something for about the hundredth time: *How to quit oxycodone*.

I already know all this stuff. Give me something new I can use, internet. Please?

When I read the words *Oxycodone can be habit-forming*, I want to punch my fist through the computer screen. Habit-forming? Like it's the same as biting your nails or picking your nose.

Fuming, I try another search: *How to make someone quit oxycodone.*

Again, just a bunch of information I already know—help lines and treatment centers and hospitals. I've called the help lines and treatment centers. They always want to talk to an adult, of course. The other day I even tried making my voice really deep and assuring them I was a fully grown adult. They sounded suspicious, but then they told me a bunch of stuff about wait times and cost and insurance that left me with the car-crash feeling.

I type in something new today: *Get into a drug treatment center when you have no money.* But all the websites and information and phone numbers that pop up make the car-crash feeling worse.

Mom and I were in a car accident a couple of years ago. We'd stopped at a red light, and Mom was asking me what we should do for dinner, McDonald's or Hamburger Helper? The light turned green, and I looked at Mom to tell her we should go to McDonald's. We had a coupon for buy-one-get-one-free

Happy Meals, and Mom always gave me the toy in hers, which meant two toys for me—total score. When I used to be into that sort of thing.

But as Mom started rolling forward into the intersection, I noticed that an old brown truck coming from the other direction seemed to be going really fast. As it got closer, I knew for sure it wasn't going to stop, and this feeling shot right through my body, forcing out all my breath and words, leaving me completely frozen. Mom turned her head to see what I was looking at, but she didn't have time to react.

I'll never forget those few seconds when I knew the truck was going to hit us—that car-crash feeling I got in my stomach and chest and throat and even in my arms and legs. Because ever since the accident, I get that feeling a lot. It's like when you trip or lean back in a chair and know you're going to fall. Or when you sit down at your desk and realize you forgot to study for a big test. Or when you're walking down the hall at school, just staring at your ugly old shoes, not bothering anyone else in the whole world, and you hear "Snaggletooth" or "White Fang."

When it hits me, my brain and body vibrate painfully, like I'm being electrified, which somehow makes me feel like I could faint and explode at the same time. I can't seem to ever get totally rid of it, so I do my best to stuff the car-crash feeling into little boxes, which I store away inside.

But I'm collecting so many boxes at this point that I worry about the day I won't have room for any more. I don't have endless storage like a big fancy house. My storage space is more like one of those hoarder houses on this TV show Mom watches. And like the hoarder houses on TV, my insides keep getting more and more cluttered and uncomfortable and stuffed to bursting. I could probably use one of those clutter experts.

Addie's video finally pops up, and I relax into my seat. Even when the car-crash feeling eases, as it's doing now because I get to watch Addie, I feel beat-up, shaky, and tired. I put on the bulky headphones.

"Hi there!" Addie says as always, holding her

phone toward her face, which is mostly covered by her helmet and mirrored sunglasses. "I'm Addie Earhart, and you're watching *The Desert Aviator*." She laughs. "All one of you. Hi, Jo!"

I smile and automatically cover my mouth with my hand. Looking around the library to make sure no one is watching me, I let my hand drop and hunch down in my seat.

There are some rough camera movements as Addie fixes the phone to the front of her helmet. "Well, I'm still on the lookout for the ringtail, that sneaky procyonid, so I was thinking we'd spend some time exploring a cliffside, where I think there might be a cave. I'll be on the ground today, so I got my snake boots on." Addie looks down so the camera shows her tall brown boots. "The snakes probably won't be out because it's going to get pretty hot, but I hope my boots come in handy. I've heard a snake's fangs can get stuck in them and break right off. How cool would that be?"

I think that sounds very *not* cool. Way too dangerous.

Addie jumps into her bright red ultralight and

buckles herself in. As she starts it up, I bob my feet on the library's thin, colorful carpet. I see what Addie sees—the desert coming at her faster and faster before she lifts into the air. A bushy mesquite tree stands in the distance, and I always worry Addie will run into it, but she makes it over again, and then she's soaring through the brilliant blue desert sky.

Addie flies over saguaros and palo verde trees; wide, barren sandy washes that will turn into raging rivers during the monsoons; and long, winding rivers of green, towering, full trees like cottonwoods and aspens, which are found in the desert only where the water floods during storms. Addie told me all of this. She knows a lot about the desert. I've lived in the city my whole life, so all I really know about the desert is what I've learned at school and from Addie. Our apartment complex has a few half-dead cactuses around the parking lot, and we've found scorpions inside, but that's about it.

"We'll be flying over some pretty interesting stuff," Addie yells over the loud buzz of the propeller. I point my pencil at a spot on my map where I'm pretty sure Addie begins and ends all her trips—a spot just east of a town called Bouse. I think maybe that's where she lives.

Addie flies over a ghost town she calls "Ghost Town Number One." There are a few ghost towns in the area. Checking my map, I figure she's flying over a ghost town called Signal. Addie once landed near Signal and explored it on the show. Mostly it was just an abandoned mine and scattered mining supplies. But she also ran into a diamond-back rattlesnake. I couldn't believe how she stood there talking about the snake while it rattled loudly nearby. She said she was out of striking distance, but I think that should be more like five miles, not five feet.

Addie lands her ultralight in a flat open area, and I draw a small star on my map where I think she is. She hops out of her ultralight and lets out a cry. "Look at that!" she squeals. "A wild pig!" Addie chases the pig, and I want to shout, *Stop! It might maul you to death!* But luckily it's far too fast for her.

"Darn," she pants before explaining how she

knows it was a wild pig and not a javelina. "Those pigs are destructive to the desert and shouldn't be here. People brought them in, and now they run wild all over the place. You don't even need a hunting license to kill one because Game and Fish wants them gone so badly."

I kind of feel sorry for the pigs. It's not their fault for being in the desert. They didn't ask to be brought there. And now they're being punished for it.

Addie jumps back into her ultralight after exploring the cliffside, including one small inlet, but no large cave as she'd hoped. She found a gopher snake, a centipede, a few scorpions, and even some bats hiding in a corner, but no ringtails.

"Oh well." Addie removes the camera from her helmet and sighs into it. "We'll just have to keep looking. Right, Jo?"

"Right," I say, and then I feel stupid, glancing around to make sure no one heard me. Everyone is still focused on their own screens.

"It's awfully hot today." Addie removes her sunglasses and wipes her eyes with the back of her hand. For a brief moment, I get a look at her face, her freckled cheeks, her hazel eyes, the wisps of light brown hair coming out of her helmet. Then she puts her glasses back on and takes a swig from the canteen she always carries, wiping her mouth when she's done. "It's supposed to be even hotter tomorrow, so I don't think I'm going to fly."

Seeing Addie is the only thing I have to look forward to lately. What am I going to do tomorrow? I guess I'll probably come back to the library anyway, maybe work on my map or read one of my new books.

"I'm sorry to disappoint anyone watching." She studies her phone. "Still just you, Jo. It's supposed to be like one-fifteen tomorrow, and I could seriously get heatstroke. Then I could, like, get dizzy and pass out or barf while flying. Can you imagine it? The barf would shoot out." Addie dramatically throws her hand out from her mouth. "And then fly right back in my face." She whips her hand back toward her face. "Giant flying barf mess. No, thank you."

Addie's words make me feel queasy. Gross.

"Back to the sky!" Addie announces, attaching

the camera to her helmet and starting the propeller back up. "How about taking a nice little detour over the mud canyon?"

Addie only needs a short distance to get the ultralight in the air, so the open sandy area near the cliffside is perfect. I follow her route on my map as she flies around the lake once before heading toward the canyon. After flying over the canyon, Addie makes a turn, the huge winding green of the wash coming into view.

Suddenly, the loud buzzing of the propeller goes completely silent, like a switch has been flipped, and all I can hear in my headphones is the wind whooshing. It's never done that before while Addie's flying.

And I know something is very, very wrong.

"Mayday, Mayday!" Addie cries. "Coming in for an emergency landing!" The video shakes from side to side, as though Addie is whipping her head around frantically, searching for a landing spot. And then the world is spinning, the desert below a brown whirl of confusion.

"I'm coming down!" Addie cries. "I'm coming down too fast!"

I grab the monitor in both hands. The camera jerks all over the place, total chaos, and no matter how hard I grip the screen, no matter how close I get to it, I can't tell what's happening

Addie is screaming so hysterically that I can't make out what she's saying or if she's even saying words at all. She seems to be struggling to catch her breath, struggling to get a word out. "Huh," she says, which turns into a shrieking sob. "Huh, juh, huh, juh," again and again until she finally gets out what she's trying to say before hitting the ground.

"Help, Jolene!"

Sheli Walters

DUSTI BOWLING is the bestselling author of *Insignificant Events in the Life of a Cactus*, *24 Hours in Nowhere*, *Momentous Events in the Life of a Cactus*, and *The Canyon's Edge*. Dusti holds a bachelor's degree in psychology and lives in Arizona with her husband, three daughters, a dozen tarantulas, a gopher snake named Burrito, a king snake name Death Noodle, and a cockatiel named Gandalf the Grey. She invites you to visit her online at dustibowling.com.